MINN
OF THE
MISSISSIPPI

MINN
OF THE
MISSISSIPPI

WRITTEN AND ILLUSTRATED BY
Holling Clancy Holling

Clarion Books
An Imprint of HarperCollins*Publishers*
Boston   New York

DEDICATION

THIS book is affectionately dedicated to my niece, Linda Lu Mahoney. The story began, one rainy morning, in Linda's home. Long before she was up, the words began trailing from a pencil, in the room where she plays. Later on, she watched — as her mother, Gwendalin, once watched my peculiar scribblings.

Gwen was not an enthusiastic herpetologist. However, she liked to watch from the roots of big walnut stumps while I waded waist-deep in the pond, capturing turtles. To help me out, she even held a few when my hands were full.

Linda likes turtles. That is, she liked the turtles brought by boys as this story got under way. Her Grandmother Lulah, from whom came half her name, found us Great-Grandmother Laura's big butter crock for a turtle pen. Linda thought it nice that I could look down at bright-eyed turtles as I typed. It was agreed that even the turtles seemed interested. Edward, Linda's father, thought that he could bring her a crockful of turtles from the Au Sable River. More or less.

Perhaps Linda never got a crockful of turtles. Perhaps she prefers to see them swimming in some pond like the pond her mother knew. That is as it should be. But the little turtles in the big crock, and the interest in Linda's eyes — all helped in the making of this book.

ISBN-13: 978-0-395-17578-1
ISBN-10: 0-395-17578-X
ISBN-13: 978-0-395-27399-9 (pbk.)
ISBN-10: 0-395-27399-4 (pbk.)

Printed in China

22 SCP 50 49 48 47 46 45 44 43 42

ACKNOWLEDGMENT

THIS is a book about a river, and a turtle in it. I thought that I knew the river well; but long residence in southern California tends to drain the memory of sustained wetness such as is found in rivers. As for turtles — hadn't I caught bushels of them in Grandfather's woodlot pond? Yet that was long ago. How long I didn't realize until, on a visit to Michigan, this book was begun. Much had been forgotten, and much I really had never known. Once again I must begin a brooding activity — "research." Once more I must go to school to rivers — and to turtles. . . .

Three boys — Thomas King, Deryl Wood and his brother Freeman — found turtles for me to meet. While hearing Clifford Ward recount years of snapper observation, my memory-gears slipped into high. Ken (now Dr. Kenneth) Prescott loaned his field notes and photographs. His patient checking of countless details, with assists from zoological friends at the University of Michigan Museum, helped me greatly.

At the Chicago Museum of Natural History (entitled "Field Museum" when I worked there), Dr. Karl P. Schmidt, Curator of Zoology, advised me on sources. Mr. Clifford H. Pope later read parts of my manuscript. John Moyer, taxidermist, and his wife Helen, provided much cheerful help. Any inaccuracy in this book is my own fault.

Friends with whom I have traveled and camped in California came bravely to the rescue. Roger P. Dalton answered questions on erosion. H. Paul Keiser explained technicalities of dams. Sidney D. Platford sent books, maps, charts, diagrams, at slightest hint of need. Hugh W. Shick added his lore of the south and its river frontiers. Dr. Frederick W. Hodge, Director of the Southwest Museum, verified Indian data. Arthur A. Woodward, Curator of Anthropology at Los Angeles Museum, brought books, pamphlets, magazines, from his personal library; worked out old trade routes; and found badly needed material on the operation of Mississippi keelboats.

Other friends furnished localized Mississippi material. Don and Helen Clancy of Detroit, Mrs. Carl L. Cramer and her mother, Mrs. Charles J. Johnson of Bemidji, Minnesota, sent headwaters data. Mrs. Frederick Addison Warner, formerly of Minneapolis, loaned documents on the north. Mrs. Harold L. Bickel of Pasadena, California, reviewed memoranda on the south, while her father, Mr. William L. Banks, told anecdotes from his interesting life along the Lower Mississippi. Mrs. Lawrence K. Thompson of Memphis contributed Delta information, and interpretations of river problems. Mr. Eugene T. Dupont of Houma, Louisiana, introduced Mrs. Holling and me to the Cajun country. Sam Mead and Lawrence Jackson, Negroes from Greenville, Mississippi, talked long about the River they had always known. And in their talk I heard again the high-water snarl, low-water chuckle and swirlings in the swamp. . . .

Three atlases were used: *Encyclopedia Britannica World Atlas,* *Goode's School Atlas, Rand McNally Road Atlas.* The Mississippi River Commission, Corps of Army Engineers, sent from St. Louis the Upper River — from Vicksburg the Lower River — in albums of maps, an inch to the mile; and pamphlet material used in some marginals.

Among herds of books consulted were *The Mound Builders* by Henry C. Shetrone; *Upper Mississippi,* Walter Havighurst; *Lower Mississippi,* Hodding Carter; *A-Rafting on the Mississip',* Charles E. Russell; *Lanterns on the Levee,* William A. Percy; *Shantyboat* — in which Mr. and Mrs. Lichty floated downriver; *Mississippi Stern-Wheelers* — an album of rare photographs compiled by Captain Frederick Way, Jr.; *Towboat River* — new photographs and a masterpiece of comment by Edwin and Louise Rosskam; *Mississippi Panorama,* cleverly edited by Perry T. Rathbone of City Art Museum, St. Louis; and, of course, the fabulous writings of Mark Twain.

Turtle books: The work of Louis Agassiz is still source material. *The Reptile Book,* Raymond L. Ditmars, is bright with photographs of turtles and reptile relatives. *Turtles of the United States and Canada,* Clifford H. Pope, is fun to read.

Librarian friends, especially those of the Pasadena Library, have kindly hunted for my many research needles in bookstacks. Abigail and her brother, F. William Johnson, permitted long use of their father's reference library. Mr. Lloyd of the Hollywood Aquarium allowed us to photograph turtles, and provided a small snapper which was soon turned from book-specimen to family pet by Mrs. Holling.

Lucille Webster Holling has watched heaps of data, note pages, color-smeared paper and pencil smudges crawl into one more book. She has wisely advised. She has endured while my "just-a-minute" dragged on into hours. Yet, while I juggled words and colors, she made a house. She designed it, drew all plans, built a model complete with furniture. Now, as this last part of the whole book clicks off my keys, the foundation slab is laid, the house is beginning to grow behind three tall palms. Friendly mountains are near. Before us gleams a far-off ribbon of sea.

The first time we met, we planned a possible trip down the Mississippi. Since then we have traveled much, but not down the Great River. We have known this vast waterway at both ends and at many points along its length, but the big trip down is for the future. Meanwhile we shall let Minn take the long journey for us. . . .

In this book I have invented word-pictures — terms such as "On-Top-River," "Water-Wall," "Dug-Ditch-River" and "Built-Up-River." To my knowledge these have not been used before. They make it a little easier for a young reader to understand how the great Mississippi runs, and how a turtle traveled with it across America.

THE AUTHOR

CONTENTS

1. LAND OF ANCIENT WATERS

THE old crow, sitting on the dead pine's tip, knew these great North Woods. For years he had flapped and soared over northern Minnesota. Each spring he beat his black wings northward — finding his forests, lakes and scattered farms unchanged. Yet this region that the old crow knew so well had been changed and re-changed in its ancient past; and each new change erased tracks of the last, like waves on sand. . . .

The old crow wouldn't have given a feather for such far-gone happenings. At this winter-ending time the country was wet. Feeling a raindrop on his beak, he cawed and flapped from his naked pine to a shaggy spruce tree. The wetness was coming again!

Big drops pelted into the spruce and found the crow. Swinging his tail, he batted a drop into shimmering mist. But it was no use — the very air was full of water! He hugged his tattered black robe tighter, closed his eyes and waited for what might come.

It came by barrelfuls. It drenched the trees. It frothed on the ground, hissing through old pine needles. The whole North Woods was a sopping sponge. Waterspouts dribbled from beak and tail of a soggy crow. . . .

This North was a land of ancient waters. After volcanic heat had cooked rock crystals into granite, waters had come. Millions of rains ground granite surfaces into soils of sand and clay. Oceans covered these soils. Sea-beds of sand were slowly compressed into sandstone, while clays and mud made shale. Shells of small sea-animals, thick on the ocean floors, turned into limestone. For millions of years, seas came and rolled away. Great heat returned, to stir and fold the rocks. Rains fell and drained off — until great coldness came. Then rains became snow, which did not melt. Ages of snowfalls packed into solid ice-sheets. The growing weight of ice pushed these glaciers outward, inch by inch. They plowed through layers of sea-laid stone, crushed fire-granite mountains. Towering ice-cliffs carried countless tons of rock. Then the glaciers melted. They left vast drifts of boulders, gravel, sand and dust across this Northland. Green plants spread slowly beside new lakes. Trees grew again on new hills. At long last, one spruce tree held a wet crow waiting for this latest deluge to end. . . .

8

The old crow had no words for talking, but he made plenty of sounds. He croaked "CAW?" which might mean "Can-It-Be?" and "CAW-AW!" or, "Rain-Has-Stopped!" Walking a wet limb gingerly, he tried out his wet wings. They still worked! Shrieking "CAW! CAW! CAW!" in great glee, he flung his body into space, beat his way to the dead pine's tip, and sat like a black carving mounted against a sun-gold cloud.

The marsh and lake below him had come alive. Blackbirds sang; mallard ducks swam; a leaping bass sent ripples ringing out against a point of sand. "CAW!" laughed the crow, dropping toward a large, dead pickerel, tossed up by waves on the sandy point, its tail in water. As he landed, a near-by lily-pad raised upward. Beneath bulged a reptile snout and two expressionless eyes. The crow and the turtle stared at each other across the dead fish. The crow began eating. . . .

Far over the lake sounded a great cawing. Black shapes whirled from the sky to cluster in trees. The old crow knew that crowd! He leaped up and flew in widening circles, screaming in crow-sounds "HEY FELLAS! LOOK! FOOD FOR ALL!" But even as he shouted, the turtle's jaws shot forward and snapped on the pickerel's tail. The fish was dragged down, and eaten under water.

Later that season, the bird and the reptile both made nests. The turtle's nest was streamlined — the bird's was an untidy heap. The old crow and his mate teased twigs together, nudged and twined them on a limb of the pine, far up from the ground. The six eggs might appear unsafe, about to roll from the nest's grass lining and be dashed to pieces. But they didn't. Too many crow generations had built rickety-looking but deep, safe nests before — and crows still flew.

The crow nest was an open platform. The turtle's nest was a buried bowl. Crow eggs would hatch only with constant care, warmed by a feathered breast, wind-protected by wings, rain-proofed by the whole spread-out body of a brooding crow.

The turtle had merely scooped a pit in the sandy beach, laid her eggs, scraped sand over them, and then had gone hunting for food. She would not return. She would never know her own children. The old crow, with a keen taste for turtle eggs, had tried to find them. But the reptile's buried secret remained hidden from a hungry bird.

CROSS-SECTION OF THE
SNAPPING TURTLE NEST
THE EGG

SNAPPERS LAY ROUND
EGGS UP TO 1⅛ INCHES.
SNAPPERS ALSO LAY
OVAL EGGS1¼ IN. LONG.
THIS IS AN AVERAGE EGG.

THE SEED

YOLK

WHITE OR
AL·BU·MEN

EACH CELL SPLITS
INTO TWO CELLS.
MILLIONS PILE UP
TO BUILD A TINY
EM·BRY·O.

THE YOLK ABSORBS
THE ALBUMEN AND
FILLS THE SHELL.

BLOOD VESSELS FEED THE
EMBRYO ITS YOLK-FOOD.

THE EMBRYO GROWS THROUGH MANY
STAGES—WORM-LIKE, FISH-LIKE,
AM·PHIB·I·AN, REPTILE STAGES, TO
BECOME A BABY TURTLE.

AS BLOOD CARRIES THE
YOLK-FOOD INTO BODY,
YOLK SHRINKS AND
TURTLE GROWS.

DRAWN WITHOUT
MEMBRANES, TO
SHOW GROWTH

Three dozen eggs, like rubbery ping-pong balls, crowded the bowl of the turtle nest. Inside the shell of each egg lay mystic silver, called by mere humans the "white." Within this floated a golden ball, the "yolk." And in this, like a jellyfish hung in a sea, a soft seed waited to grow in its dark, round, still ocean.

The sun's heat beat through the sand to the buried nest. Warmth spread down through all the eggs, layer by layer, to the very bottom egg — and crept through that shell to the soft seed hidden there in friendly darkness. The warmed seed started to swell. A strange and mysterious life bulged this seed till it pulled apart like one fat raindrop splitting into two. As if longing for company these two "cells" also swelled and divided, piling up more — all bulging and splitting. Thus these cells were growing and multiplying in their mysterious sea-within-a-sea.

These cells were not piling themselves for no purpose. They were adding new chains of cells within their secret ocean because the life in them held a memory. It remembered patterns laid out when the world was young. And, as though the Life had been given a definite, detailed task — "THESE CELLS SHALL BUILD TO A CERTAIN PATTERN WITHIN THIS SEA" — all cells were busily obeying this magic, mysterious order.

They strung themselves together like beads, making a worm — yet this was no worm. They piled on more cells until the form was fish-like, yet it was not a fish. The form became frog-like, yet it was no frog. Then it was like a reptile — and it *was* a reptile, but of a special kind. Cells spread themselves into a shield curving over a *turtle;* a *snapping* turtle; a *female* snapping turtle. And there the pattern ended. In all the universe of this round egg, there was no memory of a shape beyond this — only a well-hidden hint of what the future might hold. . . .

From nothingness a delicate, powerful Life had fed upon the inner egg. Fluid food had swelled this Life till it crowded its round, dark ocean. Now tight-curled within its shell, it could grow no larger. Something must burst so that this Life might continue growing in a wider world. . . .

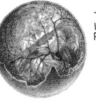

THE TURTLE GROWS   10
INSIDE A POUCH OF
PROTECTING MEMBRANES.

THIS MATERIAL HAS BEEN RE-DRAWN FROM THE
BOOK, "EM·BRY·OL·O·GY OF THE TURTLE" BY THE
FAMOUS NATURALIST, LOUIS AGASSIZ (ĂG'-Ȧ-SE)-1807-1873.

THE SMALL "EGG TOOTH"
HELPS CUT THE SHELL,
AND IS SOON OUTGROWN

2. ONE SMALL TURTLE, TWO BIG BOYS

THE turtle eggs bulged in the bowl of their sandy nest. Each egg was a home no longer, but a prison. And each prisoner, pushing and banging with his nose, was battering down his walls. It was each turtle for himself in a dash for freedom!

White eggshells burst outward. Wet walls stretched and were ripped apart under clawing feet. Freed but feeble, turtles like animated coins scrambled upward, tearing other hatching eggs, trampling unknown brothers and sisters in sandy darkness. Thus the buried treasure came alive. Fat, round, lumpy coins edged up slowly, spilled out of the sand, and wobbled downhill on flabby new feet toward water.

The old crow usually kept track of that sandy point as he sat on his pine lookout. Of late, though, he had helped rear his own troublesome family. Among most bird-tribes, the tiresome nesting season does finally end, the wobbly young ones learn to fly, and look out for themselves. Then old birds have time to fiddle with their feathers and make themselves neat again. Crows, however, get little rest. Their young, grown huge and flying strongly, still tag after tired parents for weeks on end. Now this weary crow was in quite a dither.

In the midst of neighborly conversation, a ball of black feathers barged through the scenery, knocking down leaves. The old crow could not forget, like a turtle; alas, he knew his own child! It clutched the limb he sat on and edged up to his elbow — a fluffy, wide-open valve of shrieking hunger! So the worried parent tore off through the hemlocks to find something, quickly! Beetles? Yes — but oh, the endless trips, hauling enough of them! That frog down there — it might last a choked moment — but no, it jumped. . . . Then the crow did a mid-air handspring with his wings. He saw, far off on the sandy point, many dark dots moving! Enough soft-shelled, meaty young turtles to stoke a yawning crow-child into stuffed silence!

Yet, even as he started for the point, the old crow dived into safe timber. Ah, the pity of it — his child, croaking hungrily; out there, young-turtle-food for an entire family; but down below, a tall boy with a terrible thunder-stick!

The old crow was angry. He scuttled from thicket to thicket, eyes ablaze. He paced along tangled tree branches peeking, peering. That two-legged THING, bird-like in walking but the crow's bitter enemy, could not be seen! Was it safe to go now? Yet, safe or not, those dots on the sand were disappearing! One by one, they slid into the lake. The crow could stand it no longer. Sailing far out, he swung back to the point. Swooping on the last diving turtle, in his haste he banged into wet, foam-edged sand. And his beak scooped only water!

This, however, was the *next* to last turtle. The bottom egg had hatched with the others, but this female snapper had had a longer journey out of the nest. Battling upward through cast-off shells, she was tired. Now the crow saw her, climbing out of the sand, blinking in sunlight. He hopped up, wheeled and dived.

A rifle barked. The crow lost a tail feather, and flew away fast. The rifle barked again, and a bullet skipped the small turtle like a chip over the water. The bullet had cut off her left rear leg — yet the tiny creature scarcely knew about legs. This sudden pain was possibly just a part of coming into an odd, new world.

The baby turtle had been born with a certain know-how called "instinct." From millions of past turtle-generations, rules on what to do and when were somehow recorded on the wires of her nerves. When signals came, she obeyed them. At a soundless "BREAK OUT" signal she had torn herself free from her shell. An impulse to "CLIMB UP" had urged her out of the sandy nest. "GO TO WATER" had sent brothers and sisters scurrying, but for her this one order had been blotted out by the rifle bullet. After spinning in air and splashing in water, a new signal seemed waiting there, commanding "DIVE!" She paddled down, down to muck made of decayed leaves, lily roots and rotted wood. Then "DIG!" and her tiny front feet flew.

All this haste, born of ancient fears, was automatic but necessary. A sleek pickerel, lazily cruising, had not heard the other small turtles slipping silently into his lake. When this last one splashed, he wheeled and charged. Yet he came from a mud-cloud with nothing, angrily flapping his great, wide gills to rid them of sand and woody particles. He found none of three dozen new turtles, all obeying a secret "STAY HIDDEN!"

13

THE EGG-YOLK LEFT WHEN THE
BABY HATCHES IS CALLED A "FOOD-SAC."
IT IS IN HIS WAY ON LAND, BUT IN WATER
HE DOES NOT MIND IT

The big fish did not return. In a few days the little snapper felt no more pain. An Indian boy found her floating under a lily-pad. He carefully held her by the tail.

"HO!" he laughed. "Caught you, papoose! Plenty snappy, too! Huh — one leg gone, a nick in th' shell! Somebody shoots baby snappers! Thinks he's a BIG HUNTER! But I'd hate to be him when th' Forest Rangers catch him shootin' in this Itasca State Park!

"You see, Turtle — my friends th' Rangers, they explain things. Me, I see wonderful things in th' woods, but plenty I don't understand. Like that sack on your bottom shell. I ask 'em, 'Why do baby turtles bulge out?' An' my friends say, 'Sack of food. It fed 'em inside th' egg. When they hatch, it's a food-pack.' An' I laugh. 'Food-pack — on th' *stomach? I* carry *mine* on my *back!*' They say, 'Sure, an' you stop to camp, make fire, fix food, cook it — all before you *eat.* But when baby turtles get hungry, up comes food direct! Supply lasts for days, then empty sack drops off.'

"An' I ask about breathin'. I say, 'Turtles can't breathe under water like fish, but snappers stay down for hours. Me, I feel of my ribs, my dog's ribs, my horse's ribs. Ribs pump lungs up an' down, so we breathe. When I find white old bones of turtle shells, I see th' top shell has ribs — but grown solid to it, like rafters under a roof.' An' th' Rangers say, 'Sure! Turtles can't pump their ribs! But their shoulder bones an' hip bones are still loose, so those pump their big lungs. A few breaths at th' surface, keeps 'em for hours or days. An' buried in mud all winter, they don't breathe.'

"But you, Little Turtle — you won't be breathin' long! Something will eat you! Can't swim fast — only *three* baby legs! Here, stay in this old can till I get back!"

The boy disappeared in brush. He returned with a battered old berry basket and a piece of mat from a deserted Indian camp. With a rock he sank the basket near shore, its top above the surface, and covered its bottom with muck and old leaves. He bent lily-pads to float inside the basket. Into this cage he slid the small snapper, saying, "How you like a *private* lake? This old mat makes a lid — I tie it an' cover it with water lilies. Now big fishes or that crow up there can't get you. I'll come again!"

ANY DEEP PAN CAN BE
A TURTLE-TANK

14

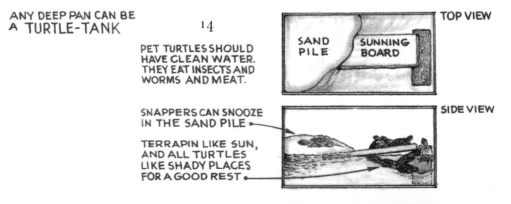

PET TURTLES SHOULD
HAVE CLEAN WATER.
THEY EAT INSECTS AND
WORMS AND MEAT.

TOP VIEW

SAND
PILE

SUNNING
BOARD

SNAPPERS CAN SNOOZE
IN THE SAND PILE

TERRAPIN LIKE SUN,
AND ALL TURTLES
LIKE SHADY PLACES
FOR A GOOD REST

SIDE VIEW

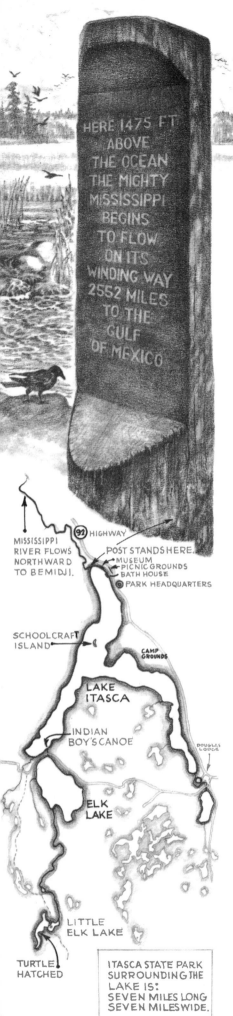

3. A TURTLE STARTS TRAVELING

THE Indian boy soon returned to his turtle-pen. He caught the small snapper under the mat lid, as it started a frightened dive.

"Too slow, Little Turtle! Ha! You've lost your food-pack, so you're not such a baby now. Stop snappin' at your friend! Say — th' Rangers found your enemy — anyhow, a tall boy, shootin' in th' Park. Took his rifle away — an' he's got to pay a big fine!

"Listen, Little Turtle! Can't hide in this pen all your life. But you're too slow — too many hungry things waitin' around this peaceful, quiet Little Elk Lake. Know where I'm goin'? With th' Rangers, a hundred miles down th' Mississippi! In canoes, checkin' up on wild life. So slide in this bait can an' come along!"

The boy followed a swamp trail. On all sides, bright lakes sparkled like mirrors laid among the marshes. Now and then the boy looked down at the can he carried, talking to the little turtle inside.

"All these lakes an' swamps start th' Mississippi River rollin' — like a sponge leakin' water. My people, Chippewa Indians, always hunted an' fished an' picked berries 'round here. Then white men began comin' — huntin' for th' 'HEADWATERS OF TH' MISSISSIPPI'! When Mr. Schoolcraft came to Lake Itasca, a hundred years back, he named it from words meanin' 'TRUE HEAD' of th' Big River. But other men still talked an' argued. Whichever water was highest *above* Lake Itasca, they said was th' *real* head!

"My people made little jokes around their campfires. They had watched surveyors, all wet an' muddy up to their beards, measurin' swamps which *might* be higher'n th' one before. My Great-grandfather, young then, he guided some surveyors. One rainy day he runs into a surveyor's tent an' yells, 'You say ELK LAKE is higher'n LAKE ITASCA? Me, I find *LITTLE* ELK LAKE higher'n ELK! No, don't go measure it yet! Me, I find *pond* higher'n LITTLE ELK LAKE! No, don't go. I find *little spring* higher'n pond! Hey, wait! I find *big tree* growin' over spring. Way up on top, I see CROW a-sittin'! Rain pourin' off both ends of crow! *NOW* — EVER'BODY RUN QUICK AN' MEASURE WHICH END OF CROW IS HIGHER'N OTHER END! AN' *THAT* IS TRUE BEGINNIN' OF MES-SIPI, GREAT FATHER OF WATERS!'"

A CALENDAR OF THE
UPPER MISSISSIPPI

16

1660 PETER RADISSON HEARS WISCONSIN INDIANS MENTION THE "GREAT RIVER."
1665 FATHER ALLOUEZ (A-LOO-ÁY') HEARS GREAT RIVER CALLED "MES-SIPI."
1673 MARQUETTE AND JOLLIET DISCOVER "UPPER MISSISSIPPI" IN WISCONSIN.
1679 FATHER HENNEPIN NAMES "ST. ANTHONY'S FALLS" (NOW IN MINNEAPOLIS).
1680 DULUTH CANOES DOWN THE ST. CROIX FROM L. SUPERIOR TO THE MISSISSIPPI.
1806 ZEBULON PIKE REACHES LEECH LAKE.
1820 LEWIS CASS (GOV. OF MICHIGAN) FINDS CASS LAKE AND ITS MISSISSIPPI INLET.
1823 GIOCOMO BELTRAMI, ITALIAN, ALMOST FINDS MISSISSIPPI'S SOURCE.
1832 HENRY R. SCHOOLCRAFT DISCOVERS LAKE ITASCA, NAMES IT FROM THE
LATIN "VER-**ITAS CA**-PUT" OR "TRUE HEAD." HE CAMPED ON SCHOOL-
CRAFT ISLAND. HIS BOOKS ON INDIANS GAVE HENRY W. LONGFELLOW
MOST OF THE MATERIAL FOR HIS BOOK-POEM, "HIAWATHA."

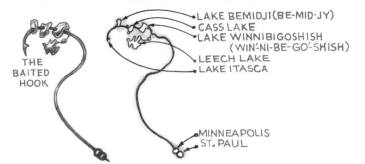

LAKE BEMIDJI (BE-MID-JY)
CASS LAKE
LAKE WINNIBIGOSHISH (WIN'-NI-BE-GO'-SHISH)
LEECH LAKE
LAKE ITASCA

THE BAITED HOOK

MINNEAPOLIS ST. PAUL

MINN STARTS DOWN MISSISSIPPI ALL ALONE.

L. SUPERIOR

THE HOOK
THE SINKER (LAKE PEPIN)

UPPER MISSISSIPPI

THE MAIN LINE

L. MICHIGAN

THE MIDDLE MISSISSIPPI

MISSOURI RIVER, GREAT WESTERN SIDE-LINE

OHIO RIVER, GREAT EASTERN SIDE-LINE

LOWER MISSISSIPPI

NEW ORLEANS

THE HUNGRY GULF OF MEXICO

In an hour the boy was paddling his canoe, saying, "Easier ridin' — huh, Little Turtle? Elk Lake's behind us. You're on Lake Itasca, head of Mes-sipi' as my people called it. Great-grandfather couldn't read words, but he sure knew maps! Said to me, 'Indian remembers *picture* map makes! Mes-sipi makes pictures of Hook-an'-Line, upside-down! See, Big-Medicine-Hook — lakes on it for bait — catches waters for th' hungry Gulf of Mexico. "Lake Pepin" makes th' sinker. Missouri River an' Ohio River are two biggest side-lines tied to big Mes-sipi line.' So, Turtle, I never forgot that map!"

As they passed Schoolcraft Island, the boy dropped a water-bug into the turtle's can. "Better learn to hunt, papoose! Up ahead is Park Headquarters — an' I hear th' Rangers startin' th' motors! We'll canoe north down th' River by outboard motor, but for quiet work we paddle. They take me along to find th' hidden places — where deer tracks tell about new fawns; beaver tracks talk about beaver. We'll read otter tracks; figure th' wild rice crop; take movies of ducks. You, Turtle, are like this River — three legs, an' th' River has 'UPPER,' 'MIDDLE' an' 'LOWER' parts. Like to travel it?"

Thus the small turtle, on waters which had once rippled her own Little Elk Lake, rode in a canoe from the north end of Lake Itasca. What she followed was at first only a brook, though the sign called it the Mississippi, starting its "TWO THOUSAND FIVE HUNDRED FIFTY-TWO MILES TO THE GULF OF MEXICO." A very young reptile rode on a very young river, in a can at the shaded bow-end of the boy's canoe. In the next weeks she traveled more than a hundred miles. She crossed Lake Bemidji, Cass Lake, Lake Winnibigoshish (winni-be-go'-shish), "Lakes-For-Bait" on the "Big-Medicine-Hook" of the boy's Great-grandfather.

Then came a last day. A Ranger said, "That snapper you saved is really stronger, and big as a dollar! I see you painted M-I-N-N on her back — is that because she comes from Minnesota?"

"Yes," said the boy. "Hatched where th' Mississippi begins. Besides, MINN is Indian for 'water.' Bein' a Water-Spirit, kind of, she *might* go down th' Big River — *maybe* all th' way! . . ."

That evening, on the riverbank, he said, "Good Medicine, Turtle-Traveler! Good-bye, MINN!" And a tiny turtle limped forward on liquid moonlight, into the Mississippi. . . .

17

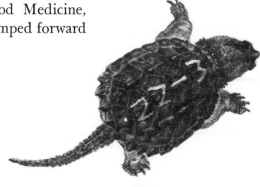

RACCOONS.
HUNTING FOR
CRAWFISH

MINK

OTTER

Minn the turtle was rather small for this Mississippi! For miles she was a chip caught in rapids and falls. When her tiny rear leg tired, she would drift — until, WHACK! Then she would push away from the boulder, and paddle again. She fought to a shore, a brook and a marsh. After a few weeks of life, Minn felt like a battered old turtle!

She came alive when a crawfish tweaked her side. Her angry, baby strike sent her enemy backward. Crows eyed its string of watery mud-clouds puffing along the brook. A raccoon family saw the mud-smoke, and came crawfish hunting. They sat in water, gazing at nothing, feeling under boulders. A sleek otter swirled by like a shadow.

Ducks hurtled out of the sky — ripping the surface with spread feet skidding. To Minn they were monsters, hinged at the surface, plunging their heads straight down. They ate bugs and beetles, at times nibbling Minn's rubbery toes with iron-hard beaks. As the air of the wild-rice swamp grew cooler, the sky was fairly a-rustle with leaves and more flying birds. Now spearheads of ducks and long-necked geese flashed by; and a mile up in the clear blue, a ghostly, shimmering ribbon of wild white swans.

Flocking crows dotted the trees, cawing, shouting, shrieking, shattering the silence. Some decided to stay on into winter, but not the old crow, whose air-trail southward lay above this marsh. He *hated* cold! With old cronies he flapped away.

Little Minn felt numb. A cold-blooded reptile, she depended on warmth of air or water to keep her active. Searching in a slow, dull way for something, she spent long moments staring at muddy bottom. She had a desire to dig in it. . . . Deeply. . . .

Muskrats towed marsh-roots to their rounded houses. Beavers stored poplar poles for the tasty bark. Otter and mink fished in ice-fringed streams. Big-footed snowshoe rabbits changed their brown coats to white. Pine squirrels flickered like running flames in the trees.

Then white flakes laid a pad over the earth to be stitched by everything moving, from mice to moose. New cold came; deeper snow. Life itself appeared to be chilled to an icy stop. Yet chipmunks and bears were only asleep. Frozen flies and mosquitoes were still living. While Minn, long since burrowed deep in the mud, was yet alive. . . .

18

MINN
HUNTS A
WINTER BED.

BEAVER

MUSKRAT

BREATHING AGAIN!

4. WATERS CAN WANDER AWAY

MINN slept through the winter, living on the air stored in her strong lungs. Now, beneath mud and water, she felt new spring warmth. Like a sleep-walker she dug her way out, floated to the surface, and breathed again. But floods hurled dazed Minn through the marsh and into the Mississippi. It was a week before she found a quiet new swamp.

The food from her food-sac, together with a few beetles and grubs, had carried her through winter hibernation. Now she was thin, weak and *hungry!* Many a wiggling thing was snapped up to make Minn bigger. Some of her hunting was done by "ambush." Under mud, unseen, her jaws snapped when food came near — and an unlucky snail or worm promptly vanished. Sometimes she hunted by walking along the swamp bottom. Several kinds of turtles are bottom-walkers, though awkward about it. Minn somehow balanced her weight so that enough of it held her down, and her rear-end limp did not matter. Slowly she walked through veils of green water like a River Spirit seeking forgotten things. Among swirling weeds, Minn with her stately, relentless tread was an ancient monster marching out of the past. Two inches of relentless monster. A born hunter.

Minn's neighbors, the pert little terrapin, buttoned themselves to logs for hours, basking in the sun. Hot, dry sunlight discourages leeches and mossy growths, so the terrapin's shells were neatly smooth. Minn preferred watery shade to sun — and so leeches became her close company, and tiny plants upholstered her shell in green velvet. This mossy coating would be shed each year. As her shell grew, spreading outward, its top layer would peel off like shreds of snapshot film, leaving her smooth and clean. Minn was deaf — yet felt even faint vibrations. She was shy — but when she looked upon her world she saw clearly, and she knew one color from another. She had much common sense.

In high water, Minn had settled in a deep pool of the swamp. When floods ran away, the pool shrank to a shallow pond. The day came when Minn's back bulged above a drying puddle, baking in the sun. Terrapin gulped food in or out of water. But Minn, a snapper, could not swallow easily except under water — and there just wasn't enough water left!

UP FROM THE WINTER SLEEP

BOTTOM-WALKING

AMBUSH

20

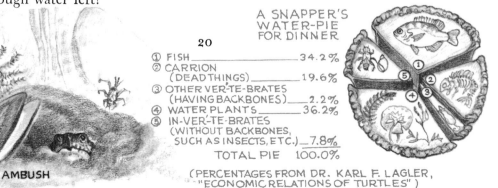

A SNAPPER'S WATER-PIE FOR DINNER

① FISH _____ 34.2%
② CARRION (DEAD THINGS) _____ 19.6%
③ OTHER VER-TE-BRATES (HAVING BACKBONES) __ 2.2%
④ WATER PLANTS _____ 36.2%
⑤ IN-VER-TE-BRATES (WITHOUT BACKBONES, SUCH AS INSECTS, ETC.) _ 7.8%
TOTAL PIE 100.0%

(PERCENTAGES FROM DR. KARL F. LAGLER, "ECONOMIC RELATIONS OF TURTLES")

Minn had no intention of starving. She splashed through scum to a baked-clay bank, and limped away. Minn on land was different from Minn in water. In a swamp she lived calmly, snapping mainly to capture food. Here, her sensitive eyes disliked bright sun; she felt mean enough to snap at anything. A porcupine met her and she hissed like a viper. The big, bristling rodent backed up as she tottered past. When a fox put down an inquisitive nose, Minn lunged at it. Her shell was less than three inches; but her neck and tail were so long that almost eight inches of angry reptile snaked forward in that strike. Though she missed and fell on her chin, the fox was impressed. When Minn arose again, an armored warrior advancing, the fox switched his plume of a tail from the brush that held it, and thoughtfully trotted off into thick ferns. After all, he *had* eaten well, this morning!

Minn's waddling took her farther away from the Mississippi. In a bubbling brook she ate happily, bottom-walking upstream. But again Minn's water-world deserted her! One day the brook stopped flowing! It gurgled and ran away, while crows fell out of the sky to feast on flopping minnows and tadpoles in the mud.

Minn scrambled to safety under draggled grass at the bank. She was confused. First, part of a wide swamp had shrunk to a puddle. Now a running brook had wandered away. Minn stared blankly about her. Then, seeming to get an idea, she started to walk. The gurgling brook had gasped, and then had run away *down*hill; yet Minn walked *up* — to a ridge of dead trees, sod and mud making a dam and a pond.

Boys who had built the dam in the brook called this place an "Ole Swimmin' Hole." Their fathers just could *not* understand how a brook, choked with boulders, poles and clay, produced better swimming than clean lakes and beaches of this summer-resort land. The boys could not explain it either — except that — well, how could you feel that a long lake *belonged* to you? While a dam — built with your own hands — it made a swimmin' hole to be proud of! Even if cows did think they owned the whole thing!

Now, dried-out Minn took over. *She* owned the swimmin' hole! She found the pool to her liking — exactly. But startled boys glimpsed a "Something" — now here, now there — and raced for help. Fathers (and sisters) came to fight this MONSTER!

21

A DAM BUILT BEAVER-STYLE

THE
PLAS-TRON:
2 BRIDGES
9 SHIELDS

A YOUNG
ADULT SNAPPER

THE
CAR-A-PACE:
5 VER-TE-BRAL SHIELDS
8 COS-TAL SHIELDS
24 MAR-GIN-AL SHIELDS
1 NU-CHAL SHIELD

4 NAILS, REAR
5 NAILS, FRONT

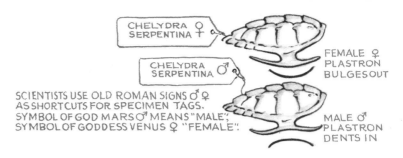

CHELYDRA ♀ ♀
SERPENTINA ♀

CHELYDRA ♂
SERPENTINA ♂

FEMALE ♀
PLASTRON
BULGES OUT

SCIENTISTS USE OLD ROMAN SIGNS ♂ ♀
AS SHORTCUTS FOR SPECIMEN TAGS.
SYMBOL OF GOD MARS ♂ MEANS "MALE";
SYMBOL OF GODDESS VENUS ♀ "FEMALE".

MALE ♂
PLASTRON
DENTS IN

A 5-INCH ADULT TERRAPIN ♀ DRAWN
TO SAME SCALE AS THE SNAPPER ABOVE

A TERRAPIN'S SOFT UNDERPARTS
ARE PROTECTED BY A LARGE
PLASTRON. A SNAPPER HAS
A SMALL PLASTRON
AND MUST PROTECT
ITSELF WITH TOOTHLESS
JAWS LIKE SHEARS.

TER.   SNAP.

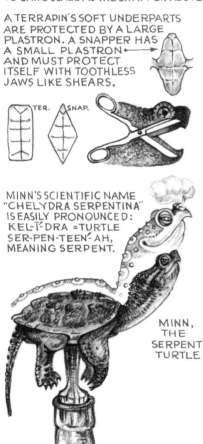

MINN'S SCIENTIFIC NAME
"CHELYDRA SERPENTINA"
IS EASILY PRONOUNCED:
KEL-Ī-DRA = TURTLE
SER-PEN-TEEN-AH,
MEANING SERPENT.

MINN,
THE
SERPENT
TURTLE

To fight this MONSTER, a father opened part of the dam. For the third time, Minn was being deserted by run-away water!

"LOOK!" piped a short boy. "I GOT 'IM! LOOKY HERE IN MY DIP-NET! A THREE-LEGGED TURTLE!"

"Huh!" said a girl, scornfully. "A MONSTER? Just somebody's pet mud-turtle! See, he had letters. Here, let me take him —— "

"No!" cried a man. "It's a female snapper — even small ones *can* bite. Painted letters have peeled off with her growing carapace —— "

"CARAPACE?" grunted another father. "Of course, you know turtles. But *what* fancy do-dad is a turtle's *carapace?*"

"Top shell. Bottom shell's a 'plastron.' They join at two 'bridges.' Divisions are 'shields.' Hand me that empty bottle."

The man-who-knew whittled a plug for the bottle, and balanced Minn upon it. Unable to touch anything, she swam furiously in air. At last she stopped, relaxed, and stared around foolishly.

"There!" cried a boy. "I *said* the head looked like a *snake!*"

"Yes, enough like one to give a scientific name of 'Serpent Turtle.' But not enough to excuse you fellows in calling it a *Monster*. Nature holds so many marvels, you don't have to stretch things!"

Someone said, "Let's paint 'er red, white and blue all over."

"No. We could re-letter her name, if we knew it. But *all over* paint would keep her carapace and plastron from growing. Her body would grow inside, squeezing her lungs, crushing her to death slowly."

"Nobody's thought of *this!*" a girl cried. "SEND HER DOWN THE MISSISSIPPI!"

And so, that weekend, they all piled into cars and made a picnic of sending Minn down the River. But a boy said, "It's so silly! Just for a dumb turtle!"

"Yes," said the man-who-knew, "turtles do seem foolish. But they *have* kept alive on this jumpy planet for a long, long time — at least some *one hundred seventy-five million years!* As one of them might say, 'We turtles saw the great dinosaurs come — and also go. And what are you, who call yourselves Humans? You haven't yet learned the simple rule — KILL ONLY FOR REAL NEED! You're a new experiment. My children's children will see how the experiment turns out — ten million years from now!' . . . "

LONG AGO, ONE KIND OF REPTILE
LIVED INSIDE HIS RIBS BECOMING
A TOUGH-CRUSTED SANDWICH.
FOR MILLIONS OF YEARS TURTLES
HAVE REMAINED AS SANDWICHES,
BUT THEY HAVE CHANGED SIZE,
SHAPE AND FEET FOR DIFFERENT
WAYS OF LIVING. THERE ARE
THREE MAIN TYPES

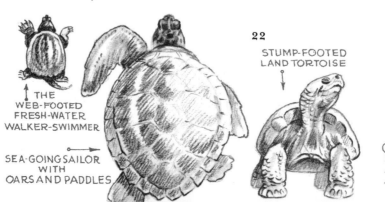

THE
WEB-FOOTED
FRESH-WATER
WALKER-SWIMMER

SEA-GOING SAILOR
WITH
OARS AND PADDLES

STUMP-FOOTED
LAND TORTOISE

22

ANCIENT TURTLE WITH
PLANT-EATING DINOSAURS:
HUGE BRONTOSAURUS
(BRON-TOW-SO'-RUS OR
"THUNDER REPTILE") AND
STEGOSAURUS (STEG'-O-
SO'-RUS, "ROOFED LIZARD").
THE PTERODACTYL, OR
"WINGED FINGER" REPTILE,
SOARS OVER TREE-FERNS
AND CYCADS (SĪ-KADS).
(READ "BEFORE THE DAWN OF
HISTORY" BY THE FAMOUS
ARTIST, CHARLES R. KNIGHT,
AN EXPERT ON DINOSAURS)

5. THE MOTHER EARTH

ONCE more Minn was a sliding chip on the slippery river. From their high sky-world, crows barely noticed this too-big-for-crow-food turtle. They saw the things she was passing, which she could not see — such as meadows (leaping with frogs); barns (caves stored with crow-corn, but tight as a clam); white houses (nests of enemies with terrible guns); and wide, smooth trails (where giant speed-bugs rolled rabbits out neatly flat for crows to feed on).

From her low-water-world, Minn saw only riverbanks passing, mile on mile: sand, gravel, clay, and always boulders — hazed over by wild rice or rushes, or blurred by willows. The sky was wide, or chopped up among trees — for this was still the North Country of forests and farms. Trails, unseen from the River, leaped over it suddenly. There were railroad trestles laying ladder-like shadows along the water — with dragons hurtling above young Minn with hoots and thunders. She drifted through solid shadows of highway bridges, where hissing reptiles passed.

At last she found a swamp she liked, and she clung to it. Next spring the floods were so spread out that they could not tear her away. Here her carapace grew to four inches. The following spring a boy captured her. He carved his initials on the edge of her horny carapace — not deeply, for he knew how tender was his own thumb under its nail. But even carved letters were outgrown, because old shields peeled off every year, leaving new shields.

The old crow would not have recognized this six-inch Minn. He soared over her swamp, now and then, on restless migrations. Though Minn and her River had circled some hundreds of miles, the old crow's pine was not a hundred miles off — "as the crow flies." He could not even remember Minn. Why should he remember a mouthful he never quite caught? And why should the almost-mouthful ever remember?

Thus Minn lived in the swamp she liked, and grew larger still. She watched as rails and plover ran on the wet mud shores. Blue herons and bitterns waded the deeper marsh. Mallard ducks swam. Minn was big enough now even to duel with ducks!

24

LEAF OF
WILD RICE
(ZĪ-ZĂ-NĬ-A
A-QUĂ-TĬ-CA)

AUTUMN EAR

GRAIN,
NATURAL SIZE

PORCUPINE
AND
CHIPMUNK

GREAT
BLUE
HERONS

MALLARD
DUCKS

PIPING PLOVERS

VIRGINIA RAIL

BITTERNS

For all her slowness and stately calm, Minn, too, was restless at times. She had her moods. As a rule she cared little for snapper company — and after one look at her open jaws, the company waddled away. But Minn was changing. Strange urges took her to shore. And there she joined other snapping turtles, lying on sand like flat stones doing nothing at all. Though she met male snappers larger than herself, she seemed to know that someday she would be larger than any mere male. She even frolicked with them in water. Two turtles faced each other, in one game, snorting out bubble-streams. Again, in games of tag, several snappers bit at feet, tails, jaws in good-humored confusion, clumsily clawing at anything that came handy. Dark bodies swirled and danced in the water like pie-plates being whirled in a washing machine. Greedy-eyed crows watched the churning surface, where feet, heads and tails splashed out and turned over like cogs in gears. *Surely* dead turtles must soon float up from those savage battles! Yet out of those ancient, mysterious games, none ever did. . . .

One morning a thick fog cloaked Minn's swamp in layers of mystery. A breeze rippled it, pried it up, lifted its veil over the rushes in tatters. And through the tatters a warm sun found a new day; a day very important for Minn, now with a grown-up, seven-inch carapace. For the day brought a new urge, sending her to shore. She *must* find a certain place! At the swamp's edge she splashed over driftwood limbs like a frying pan skidding across a giant washboard. She tipped herself like a fry-pan on edge to slide between cat-tail stalks. She fought willow shoots and tamarack fronds, floundering uphill over roots. Coming to gravel and boulders she slowed — but this was not *the* earth. Through turtle-sized brush of wild strawberry plants she pushed her way, haste and determination in every lurching movement. Until, battering down a stockade of stiff grasses, she landed bottom-up in a deer trail.

Minn pried herself over with her nose, and put on speed. Even with her teetering limp she was really traveling! Gal-lump, thump! Gal-lump, thump! How could she guess that she was a bowl of eggs moving on three legs? She knew only that she felt like bursting. She *must* get there! Where? Not here — not here — Gal-lump, thump! She *must* keep going! . . .

25

MINN DIGS HER
JUG-SHAPED NEST.

No mere human could know why Minn stopped where she did in the trail. Yet for some turtle reason, THIS was the very place! Her strong rear foot began scratching, scraping, tearing away at the ground. Two rear legs would have worked one after the other. But this one was a living spoon, digging a cavity. This bowl in sandy loam would take the place of the bowl which was her body. And, slanted like a dish set in a draining rack, Minn began to lay her eggs. At six years of age she laid eggs in the friendly earth, foster-mother of all turtles everywhere.

A curious woodchuck waddled past while Minn laid her eggs. Chickadees chirped excitedly. A buck deer, careful of tender velvet antlers in brush, leaped over her. Minn stared blankly. That leg continued to work as with a will of its own.

When a white egg left her body at the base of her tail, that foot scooped it away to the side like a gentle hand. Around and around, fourteen eggs were packed snugly in layers in the earthen bowl. By noon they were covered with earth. In a few short hours the hasty search, nest making and egg laying were completed. It was up to the mother earth now, and the sun. If no harm came, Minn's first infants would hatch in a hundred days. Then these swamps might know her descendants for thousands of years to come. As for Minn — it was over, and she was *hungry!* With never a backward glance she started for her swampy home.

The deer trail threaded its way on a "hog's-back" — a narrow rise of ground between two low places. On one side lay the swamp, on the other a trout-filled stream. Along the stream came two boys with fishpoles, and two rollicking dogs. The old collie paused only to sniff at Minn, wisely backing away from her hissing jaws. But the hound pup went wild. As though he had run down the mightiest game in all the north forests, he bayed till he almost strangled. Meanwhile he neglected to tuck up his tail. When he whirled around just right, Minn clamped down on it. The only glimpse the running boys got of her was of a roundish something skidding and bumping downhill behind a yelping young dog.

26

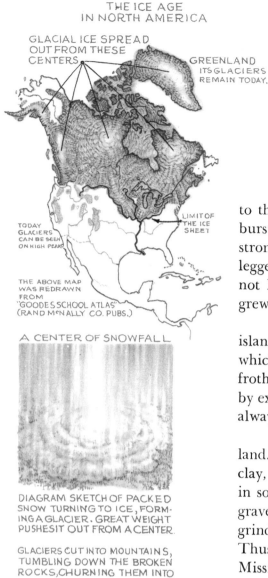

THE ICE AGE IN NORTH AMERICA

GLACIAL ICE SPREAD OUT FROM THESE CENTERS

GREENLAND ITS GLACIERS REMAIN TODAY.

TODAY GLACIERS CAN BE SEEN ON HIGH PEAKS

LIMIT OF THE ICE SHEET

THE ABOVE MAP WAS REDRAWN FROM "GOODE'S SCHOOL ATLAS" (RAND McNALLY CO. PUBS.)

A CENTER OF SNOWFALL

DIAGRAM SKETCH OF PACKED SNOW TURNING TO ICE, FORMING A GLACIER. GREAT WEIGHT PUSHES IT OUT FROM A CENTER.

GLACIERS CUT INTO MOUNTAINS, TUMBLING DOWN THE BROKEN ROCKS, CHURNING THEM INTO THE ICE AS IT CREEPS INCH BY INCH.

FOR AGES THE ICE MOVED OUTWARD, MELTED BACK LEAVING HILLS OF CRUSHED ROCK, RESURFACING THE LAND.

THE GLACIER MELTED, LEAVING "MORAINES" OR GRAVEL DUMPS.

ICE-PUSHED STONES MAKE GROOVES IN ROCK

MINN EXPLORES THE HOOK

0 10 20 40 60 80 100
SCALE OF MILES ON MAP

① MINN IS HATCHED HERE
② STARTS ON RIVER IN CANOE
③ JOURNEY WITH INDIAN BOY
④ MINN'S FIRST WINTER
⑤ MINN FINDS THE BOYS' DAM
⑥ MINN GROWS LARGER
⑦ MINN LAYS FIRST EGGS

6. THE RIVER IS A MUSEUM

MINN quickly let go of the hound pup's tail, and rolled downhill to the trout stream, where she fed greedily. The next summer cloudburst washed her back to the Mississippi again. With larger body and stronger rear leg, she still was no match for this youthful river. Four-legged snappers might bottom-walk upstream in spring migrations, but not Minn. She had to rest in shallows near shore, for now her River grew rougher.

It scooted her through a rocky gorge, while it split itself on an island. Rejoining itself it guzzled new rivers, such as the Crow Wing — which doubled its size. Whooping, it bowled Minn over boulders in frothing rapids. For two years she sought rest from the brawling River by exploring the mouths of placid streams running into it. But she was always returned to the Mississippi.

Glaciers had spread clay, gravel and big stones across this northland. Minn found rivers running on boulder beds. She might dig in clay, sand or muck, but she found boulders beneath. She entered cuts in solid granite and sea-laid stone, ground out by swirling water with gravel and sand. Though large boulders were smashed and worn by grinding, they merely became smaller boulders, more gravel and sand. Thus granite stones kept rushing rivers from digging deeper. Minn's Mississippi, though it cut gorges now and then, was here mainly a surface-flowing "ON-TOP-RIVER."

Minn liked to smell the new streams as they joined the River. Some raced from far forests tawny with wood-mold, holding a bittersweet tang of timber and roots. Some crawled from flat prairies, scented with lush green plants. Marshy creeks smelled and tasted of muck, rocky streams brought odors of granite, shale or limestone. There were strong tastes of copper and iron in this fresh, north-wilderness river.

Towns added new scents. Minn whiffed the pungent essence of sawdust from lumbering towns. Country towns provided apples, tomatoes, cabbage-leaf-leftovers. When currents smoked with such tempting aromas, Minn hunted them down. But when chemical wastes from some factory smarted her eyes, Minn was worried. She hunted and held to the forest-scented channels where these chemicals were weakest.

28

THE GLACIAL, OR PLEISTOCENE (PLIS'-TOW-SEEN) PERIOD LASTED SOME HALF MILLION YEARS, AT ITS END (12,000 TO 25,000 YEARS AGO), ITS ODD ANIMALS (LIKE THESE) DIED OUT.

MASTODON

SABER-TOOTH TIGERS

MAMMOTHS

GLACIAL DRIFT

ANCIENT LAYERS OF
WATER-LAID SANDSTONE
AND LIMESTONE

THE "STRING",
A SECTION OF
A LOG RAFT

*BURR-OAK STAPLE
*HARDWOOD PEGS
BIRCH TIE-POLE

OLD,
WASTEFUL WAY
OF "TYING" LOGS

A
"SWEEP"
AT EACH END
FOR STEERING

Minn saw mile after mile of charred logs on the river bottom. To her they were as natural as boulders. Yet, had she been human, they would have told a sad story. . . .

For ages, northern forests protected their floors with mats of wood mold. Each autumn, dead leaves drifted; winter winds heaped the fallen limbs; each spring found old trees toppled criss-cross, decaying under ferns and mosses. This dank sponge held the rains, dribbling cool water so that streams flowed steadily, even in summer.

Indian tribes lived and died, changing the forest no more than its flickering shadows. Because woodland animals provided rich furs, white traders and trappers who came next did not destroy forests. Then other men came. Axes and saws toppled the great trees down. Mississippi turtles found their river churning with logs for sawmills. Crows soared over log rafts drifting with the current or pushed by steamboats — twisting serpents of logs sometimes three city blocks long.

Northern logs furnished lumber badly needed for a nation's buildings. But in those wild days lumbering was wasteful. It was "cut and run" — leaving miles of slashings — heaped-up piles of branches, tender young saplings uprooted. Here fires started, devouring forests, gulping towns — and hundreds of people. Game perished. Birds fell dead from the skies. Blackened stumps were tombstones in vast graveyards of ashes. Even the ancient forest-sponge was seared away. New generations thought it only natural that northern streams should rage in spring — and dwindle in summer.

Farmers came to the North. Crops were coaxed from cut-and-burned lands, and cowbells tinkled merrily across blueberry barrens. Children played in fields fenced by rows of blackened, dragon-toothed stumps. Slowly young birch trees raised their white poles on sawdust mounds where hungry mills had stood. Stretches of old forest, missed by axe and fire, spread across hills. Children grew, went away to college and returned with new wisdom and a new word — CONSERVATION. They replanted wasted woodlands. When they cut old trees for timber, they planted new trees. They built dams, restocked waters with fish, brushlands with gamebirds, protected game. People who had grown up in a wasteland gave their grandchildren lakes and streams churning with fish again, and wide, green forests in which to play. . . .

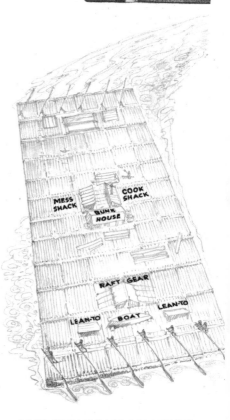

MESS SHACK
COOK SHACK
BUNK HOUSE
RAFT GEAR
LEAN-TO
BOAT
LEAN-TO

A "SIX-STRING" RAFT. SOMETIMES THE MISSISSIPPI SAW FIFTEEN-STRING RAFTS — THREE ACRES OF FINEST WHITE PINE FLOATING TO HUNGRY SAWMILLS.

29

A STUMP FENCE — THE REMAINS OF GREAT PINES 3 TO 6 FEET THICK, 100 TO 220 FEET HIGH, WHICH ONCE MADE AN UNBROKEN FOREST ACROSS MANY NORTHERN STATES. (SUCH OLD-FASHIONED FENCES ARE NOW RARE.)

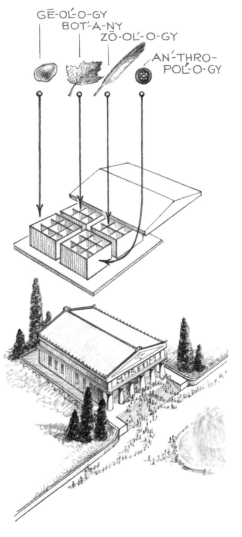

A NATURAL HISTORY MUSEUM IS SIMPLY A ROOFED GROUP OF FOUR BIG BOXES HOLDING SPECIMENS. THESE FOUR "DEPARTMENTS" WITH "DIVISIONS" HOLD FOUR KINDS OF THINGS – SPECIMENS OF OUR "EARTH" – ITS PLANTS – ITS ANIMAL LIFE – AND ITS PEOPLE. FOUR SMALL OBJECTS CAN START A MUSEUM – A PEBBLE, A LEAF, A FEATHER AND A MAN-MADE BUTTON. THESE REPRESENT THE FOUR MAIN DEPARTMENTS:

GE-OL-O-GY
BOT-A-NY
ZO-OL-O-GY
AN-THRO-POL-O-GY

Minn, though descended from one of the oldest, crustiest families on the River, knew nothing of the past. However, she lived in a museum corridor two thousand five hundred miles long. She walked among vast collections of American specimens — from ancient rocks and fossils to tin cans, airplane parts and bottle tops. Minn paused often beside heaped or laid-out museum treasures; wondering if they held food, or whether she might rest there.

The land donated many specimens to this River Museum for ge-ol'-o-gy, bot'-any and zo-ol'-o-gy departments. The zoology department held many bones. Some were bones of mice, recently eaten by owls. There were bison bones, from days remembered by the oldest buffalo hunters. There were fossil mastodon skulls from a glacial past, when elephants roamed America. And there were also an'-thro-po-log'-ical specimens — objects man had made. The latest were strewn on the floor under covers of silt — air-guns, shoes, marbles, rubber tires, bicycles, shapes of metal. Now forgotten as useless to the world of air, they were refuges for countless water creatures.

Because cities held people who threw things at turtles, Minn often went below. She walked on museum deposits before reaching a town, but larger hoards lay downstream, pushed there by currents. When Minn came to these large treasure heaps she knew it was safe to surface — the town lay upstream. Sprawled restlessly on one bank or both, it puffed, tooted, clashed its noisy importance. Minn, very hard-of-hearing, could feel its vibrations. But she viewed all towns in a reserved, thoughtful manner. Like a sober scientist weighed down with problems she would walk among shapeless monuments to the past. Minn found flint points, copper axes, pewter mugs, flintlock rifles — and even an old-fashioned, wood-burning locomotive.

While passing one day through assorted specimens, Minn felt heavy vibrations. Frothy rapids tumbled her past high buildings with glassy eyes. She did not know that she was coming to the end of her ON-TOP-RIVER — where it slid off the highest shelf in its entire length, and dropped down. Minn did not know that falls were ahead.

30

THE FALLS
(RE-DRAWN FROM A
PRINT MADE IN 1881.)

ST. ANTHONY'S FALLS
DROP 16 FEET—THEN
WITH RAPIDS, DROP 80 FEET
IN THE FIRST ONE-HALF MILE.

7. BELOW THE WATER–WALL

MINN had reached the "Falls of St. Anthony." In the past, this rock wall frothing with water had meant that Indians must "portage," or carry, their canoes and packs around it. A priest, coming upon its wilderness beauty, named it in honor of a saint. Then other people came, building sawmills for it to run. When steamboats at last puffed up the River from far-off St. Louis, they could go no farther — this "Water-Wall" stopped them. A town grew up around St. Anthony's Falls. It was named from the Sioux Indian "Minne" meaning "water," and the Greek syllables "ap-o-lis" meaning "city." And Minneapolis, City-of-Waters, used power from "The Falls" to become, among other things, the greatest grain-grinding, flour-milling city in the world.

This Water-Wall ended Minn's ON-TOP-RIVER. It began being a DUG-DITCH-RIVER. Leaping the sixteen-foot falls, it dropped eighty feet in the first half-mile. As frantic Minn fell over the Water-Wall, a young man leaned from a high-up window.

"Hey!" he yelled. "A turtle! Went over them falls! Think of floatin' down Ole Mississip! Wisht *I* was a turtle ——"

"Don't worry" — growled a man. "You're slow enough to be one! Git to work!"

Now Minn's bluff-bordered river connected two cities. Eight miles south of the Water-Wall, Minnesota River joins the Mississippi. Here, on a bluff, Fort Snelling was built to protect the wild Northwest Frontier. Steamboats landed supplies on banks near "The Fort." Warehouses, stores and trading posts were later combined into busy St. Paul.

Colonel Snelling, for whom The Fort was named, had sawmills built at The Falls, and grain mills, too. While St. Paul became known as a trader's town, Minneapolis was known as a place for making things. Thus Minneapolis, a center of manufacture, and St. Paul, a center of commerce, spread out and out like rings on a pool — creeping along the bluffs toward each other through woods and weeds. Then rough wilderness roads became neat streets, the houses of two towns meeting along them. Minneapolis and St. Paul, first linked by the River, were now "Twin Cities." Today a stranger, walking the park-shaded streets, sometimes must ask in which of the Twin Cities he might be.

32

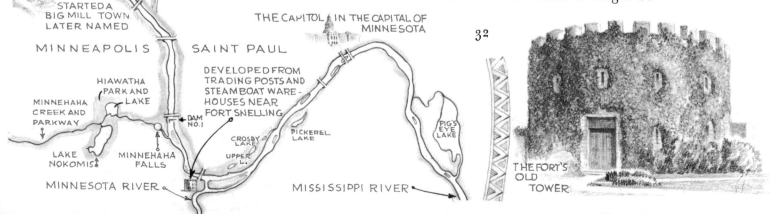

THE FORT
RE-DRAWN FROM A
PRINTED SKETCH BY
HENRY LEWIS (1846 OR 48)

OLD FORT SNELLING
(ESTABLISHED IN 1819)
WHERE MINNESOTA RIVER →
MEETS THE MISSISSIPPI

Along river-bottom between the bluffs, Minn found many relics of the Twin Cities' past. Worn wood, rock and twisted metal made torn pages of a continued story. When Minn dug in clay or currents eddied the silt, new pages of the story came to light.

Below the Water-Wall, Minn stumbled on soaked timbers hinting of log houses "modernized" with boards. In sand lay rusty, snag-toothed saws, worn from gnawing through miles and miles of logs. Minn found cracked millstones which had ground tons of flour. These told of grainfields crowding teepees and Indian ponies from the prairies.

Minn passed airplane props, auto tires, bicycle pedals, a buggy axle, a locomotive headlight. She nudged a steamboat's brass whistle which had blasted wilderness silence long before railroads came. Many things had plopped overboard when steamboats unloaded at these banks — axe-heads, hoes, a plow, a blacksmith's anvil — lost at a time when eager young farmers from Europe had flocked by thousands to settle this wild, new, free Northwest.

Then came pages of days before farmers — the curved blade of a knife, three beaver traps rusted together. These told tales of French and Indian trappers, and fuzzy bales of beaver fur. By silent canoes the bales had come here, by loudly squeaking prairie-carts — high "Red River Carts" hauled southward from Canada by oxen, sometimes by half-tamed buffalo. Minn found the rotted hub of a wheel from this time; and a split paddle-blade.

Minn rested beside a cracked cannon-barrel. Once it had boomed salutes — when The Fort was young, soldiers wore new uniforms, and sabers flashed on parade! When officers, ladies, in blue wool and satins, bowed and curtsied at candlelit balls. . . . "Yes ma'am! Colonel Snelling has ordered a *sawmill* built at The Falls." "How nice! Imagine — new table-tops *sawn* by *machine!*" "Yes'm, and word is that a STEAM-BOAT *might* make it clear to here, from St. Louis!" "*I swan!* I mean, I *certainly do declare!*"

Minn found other tokens; nails pounded flat for arrowheads; lead bullets; brass-bound guns. . . . And braves had come from the forest; wanting old trade-muskets mended by white man's tools. Blanketed — harmless-looking as stuffed dolls — but leaping in firelight like lean copper spears; howling across the starry night like wolves. . . .

33

MINNEAPOLIS IS A CITY OF SHADY PARKS
AND SPARKLING LAKES.

OLD INDIANS, LOOKING DOWN
FROM THE BLUFFS, WOULD NOT
KNOW THEIR MISSISSIPPI,
EDGED BY GIANT STONE
TEEPEES AT SAINT PAUL.

Minn wouldn't have given a carapace-scale for all of the Twin Cities' past. The present was good enough for her, with buns from bakeries, vegetables — and things. Though guards worked hard to keep parks clean, a few picnic lunches got lost in Minnehaha Park, leaped over Minnehaha Falls — and ended in Minn. She *liked* parks!

But Minn *hadn't* liked her fall at the Water-Wall! And a dam gave her a fright as she shot through its under-water gates! This big ditch was too noisy! Minn moved. . . .

Before she realized it, Minn had walked in her museum corridor clear out of St. Paul. She had left this Capital of Minnesota, its crowds and vibrations were gone. She was still in a ditch, but one side widened into a green-furred marsh. Above the marsh black crows flapped southward; gray geese drew wavering lines across the sky. At night, a light on a far bluff showed that some human lived there. . . .

Minn held to the marsh for the rest of that year. The next spring she found the River raging. It could cut down bluffs and rebuild them again as islands. Some islands held trees scarred by ice and logs heaved at them by floods. Floods left trees with their trunks clay-coated ten feet up; drying in neat, level lines of whitewash. Floods left brush in ghostly branches like nests of giant birds. . . .

Some bluffs were like cities, like castles, like ivy-clad cottages — but all silent and still. Green islands were braided with green roads of silent water. Rock wing-dams elbowed out from the land, just under the surface. Channels for chugging river-traffic were marked. Painted buoys and lights pointed the way through green silence. . . .

There were shantyboat people living alone till the sounds of their own voices startled them, so they spoke but little. Other lonely people were afraid of the silence; they took on the habits of running water, gabbling to themselves. Minn saw a man in a scow heaped with clamshells. "Very *next* clam," he muttered, *"will* have a *pearl* in't. But, if'n it don't — 'twill leastwise make pearly buttons. Reckon I've hauled enough shell fer whole *mountains* of buttons. . . ." Minn walked sometimes on a clay-sandy bottom paved with punched-out, lace-holed shells. . . .

34

SHANTYBOATS ARE LITTLE HOUSES ON FLAT-BOTTOMED SCOWS. THEY DRIFT DOWNSTREAM, GUIDED BY OARS. SOME HAVE MOTORS.

PEARL BUTTONS ARE BORED OUT OF A CLAMSHELL. ALONG THE MISSISSIPPI, CLAMS ARE PRODUCERS OF A FEW FINE PEARLS, AND CARLOADS OF BUTTONS. ANCIENT INDIANS STRUNG PEARLS FOR BEADS, AND INLAID POLISHED SHELLS IN THEIR SACRED CARVINGS.

8. MINN BECOMES A RIVER–MONSTER

FROM the Water-Wall, "Head of Navigation" for large steamboats, Minn traveled a winding river. She explored new marshes and islands, each summer leaving more eggs in a new nest. Her restless spirit always took her back to the River. Though she fought it, and in spring strove to edge upstream as other snappers might do, floods met and swallowed her and forced her southward again. Like the River itself, lashing back and forth between bluffs, she struggled against fate. At last her tired leg would give up to the River, and she would go almost gleefully — over wing-dams, over big dams, scooting places in a watery hurry. And she had her adventures. . . .

An elderly riverman rowed an eastern tourist along vine-clad shores. Pointing, he said "Look! Snapper with its head high up! That'un is still trustful of folks, an' ain't been hurt much, lately. But once snappers git hurt — they sure remember lessons! They git wise, an' plenty shy. A man's got to go some to outsmart 'em!"

The second autumn out of St. Paul Minn was ten years old, with a carapace eleven inches long. She forced her ten pounds into a crowded apartment. It had been a muskrat burrow in a marshy bank. As more turtles found it, each scratched at the walls, widening the burrow. When the last had arrived, Minn was layered among fifteen other snappers in the mud. Such an army left telltale signs at the door. Two turtle-hunters found the trampled entrance and dug on through.

"Sure hit the jackpot!" one chuckled, careful to lift each turtle by its long, knobby tail. "A smart haul of turtle meat for stews an' soups!" He dropped the sluggish animals into the scow for his partner to tie up in sacks. "Them restaurants will pay — le's see now. Big an' little, these will run about ten pounds dressed meat apiece — ten times sixteen is a hundred sixty pounds, at ten cents — that makes SIXTEEN DOLLARS! A few more hauls like this here, an' — hey! What *are* you doin' — TOSSIN' THAT TURTLE BACK IN TH' RIVER! HAVE YOU GONE PLUMB HAYWIRE?"

"No, I'm jest sensitive. My young brother come out of a war with one leg gone. This turtle lost th' same. I'm givin' her a chance."

36

Up to now, Minn had somehow eluded fishlines. She disliked the looks of baited hooks but, near Hastings, Minnesota, she sampled one. Without swallowing the bait as most turtles do, she snapped it up hastily, tossing her head sidewise. The hook's sharp point pierced down in her mouth, sliding through the soft middle, at the end of her lower jaw. Surprised by the sudden spurt of pain, Minn slashed blindly about her. She found nothing to fight except empty water. Then she was conscious of the hook itself. Its shank had turned over and lay half out of her mouth. Though her powerful bite could cut sticks, this thing was steel. Snapping merely left bruised notches along the cutting edge of her jaw.

The problem grew more complicated in an instant. The hook was going somewhere and dragging Minn with it. At the stubborn, relentless pull of the line, Minn went into a fury of tugging, swinging her head, whipping it about. But she had no place for a grip with her feet; she couldn't touch bottom now, there was no leverage in green water. She felt herself being drawn steadily upward on a long slant. She recognized the shadow of a boat's bottom above her — then she bumped the boat and had something to brace against. Pushing away from the boat's side with her strong front feet, she felt her head yanked above water. Now she saw her real enemy. It was not the hook, nor the line — but a man.

Except for their splashings, pole pokings and stone tossings, Minn had held no real ill feelings for men. But for this one her eyes filled with an icy glitter. A cold, reptilian hate was focused on this human. It was a forgotten hate — dredged up from the deeps of ancient swamps, formed and funneled into one piercing look, and the man holding the line taut over the gunwale felt the odd force of this gaze. It made him nervous. Those unwinking, beady eyes were staring at HIM!

He was after fish, not turtles! Why had this dumb reptile grabbed his line? He'd show the world that it didn't pay to spoil a St. Paul plumber's Saturday afternoon! He reached for his gaff and swung — but the big landing hook missed.

37

NORTH AMERICA HAS TWO SNAPPERS.
THE "ALLIGATOR SNAPPING TURTLE"
(LOCALLY CALLED "LOGGERHEAD")
SOMETIMES WEIGHS OVER 200 POUNDS.

THE
"COMMON
SNAPPING
TURTLE" (LIKE MINN)
RARELY GROWS TO WEIGH
50 POUNDS, THOUGH ONE
WAS FATTENED TO OVER
60 POUNDS.

The man's second swing of the gaff nicked Minn's carapace along its edge, then thudded into the boat's side, sticking tightly. The snapper had not moved a muscle from her open-mouthed, baleful glare. The man worked faster, prying at the gaff, trying to keep his elbows from Minn's reach, to hold the wire leader tight, to draw his eyes from that ancient reptilian stare. But all this was too much for him. He lost his balance, the boat slid over until, with a choking squawk of fear he slid headfirst down on the snapper, into the water. . . .

As he told it afterward, that snapping turtle grew in his memory. Her wide-apart jaws swelled wider in his nightmares. One eye, a windmill of frenzy, turned into a green whirlpool — in which he, his boat and a monster turtle churned 'round and around! Such visions could *not* be conjured up by an *ordinary snapping turtle!* It must have been an alligator snapper — a big "loggerhead"! And not an ordinary loggerhead, either! A full twelve inches between those awful eyes, if an inch -- a shell twice as big as the boat — and it must have weighed well over four hundred pounds! Yeah! Didn't it tip his craft easy as rolling a log? And there he was, sliding down over that reptile, feeling her sharp beak bumping his soft, unprotected stomach — it was sure a miracle he wasn't split like a melon, then and there! And what did he do? Why, he splashed and scrambled and hoisted himself on the overturned boat and lay there gasping on the slippery bottom, hauling his feet in — expecting to lose a leg any minute — talk about horror! Yes, there was something plenty uncanny about it all. Personally, he wasn't so sure that old Indian tales might not be right; there *might be* a real River-Monster! . . .

Minn had not paused for revenge. She wanted only to get away. Paddling swiftly down, she dragged line and rod. The rod caught on a snag. The line snarled across her jaws and tore off close to the leader. Under a waterlogged plank she sulked in slow fury, mouthing the steel. At last the point slid out under her jaw, and caught in driftwood; the wire leader slid through the wound, and Minn was free.

38

THIS·BLUFF-BORDERED·CANYON·RUNS·SOUTHWARD 1,000 MILES.

← ST. ANTHONY'S FALLS
(THE·WATER-WALL)

SOUTH OF THE WATER-WALL, THE MISSISSIPPI IS
"THE·DUG-DITCH-RIVER." RUSHING WATERS
GOUGED IT OUT — BUT, ACCORDING TO OLDEST
LUMBERJACKS "'TWAS PLOWED OUT, IT WAS SO,
BY PAUL BUNYAN AN' HIS SKY-BLUE OX, BABE !"

9. THE LAKE IN THE RIVER

FISHERMEN laughed. "That guy almost *swallowed* by a turtle? Scared stiff by an old *snapper! Alligator* turtles — they don't come as far north as Hastings, Minnesota!"

Right now that "old" snapper did not remember her awful experience. Dazed from churning through another big dam near Hastings, she drifted to Prescott at the mouth of the St. Croix River. Minn bumped against mossy pilings. She sank in the shade of the big dock above her. She was too dizzy to notice people on the dock.

"Yep, son," said an old-timer sitting on the dock, "you folks are now in Wisconsin. Yes, 'St. Croix (croy) is French for 'Holy Cross.' That there river divides Wisconsin an' Minnesota. Old trappers' stream, it was. French an' Injuns canoed from Lake Superior by th' short Brule (brool) River, an' down th' St. Croix. Later 'twas famous for loggin'; an' Prescott, here, was leapin' with lumberjacks every Saturday night! Prescott built fast an' fancy steamboats too. All snow-white, like floatin' castles of frosted lace!

"How's that? You heard t'other day a man was nigh eaten by a MONSTER? Shucks! We're used to monsters, in these parts. Ever hear of th' giant Paul Bunyan? Him an' his sky-blue ox, Big Babe, plowed this ditch of th' Mississippi! Yep, a thousand-mile ditch, Minneapolis to th' Ohio River. Them hills all along it — them bluffs are jest clods turned up by Paul's monster plow! Git a lumberjack goin' on such yarns, you'll soon see everything larger than natural size! But — there really *is* a River-Monster downsteam — a *lake!* An' it has swallered big boats, an' plenty of people!

"Forty-eight miles south of here is th' Chippewa River. Some thousands of years back, it dumped sand at its mouth an' dammed up th' Mississippi. Made it swell in its ditch, from bluff to bluff. At last it busted th' dam enough to keep goin' — but th' spreadout lake is still there. 'P-E-P-I-N' 'tis spelled; we call 'er 'Pippin'. Twenty miles long, by two or three. Steep bluff walls — not many good landin's fer boats, or even canoes. Mighty purty lake, she is. But many a sailor, took in by her beauty, has been mighty upset by her squally temper! Talk about winds, waves an' wrecks ——"

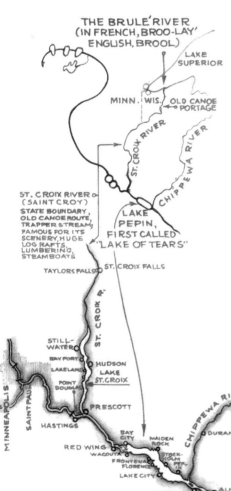

THE BRULE' RIVER
(IN FRENCH, BROO-LAY'
ENGLISH, BROOL)

LAKE SUPERIOR

MINN. WIS.   OLD CANOE PORTAGE

ST. CROIX RIVER

CHIPPEWA RIVER

ST. CROIX RIVER
(SAINT CROY)
STATE BOUNDARY,
OLD CANOE ROUTE,
TRAPPER STREAM,
FAMOUS FOR ITS
SCENERY, HUGE
LOG RAFTS,
LUMBERING,
STEAMBOATS

LAKE PEPIN,
FIRST CALLED
'LAKE OF TEARS'

TAYLORS FALLS   ST. CROIX FALLS

ST. CROIX R.

STILL-WATER

BAY PORT   HUDSON
LAKELAND   LAKE
POINT   ST. CROIX
DOUGLAS

MINNEAPOLIS   SAINT PAUL

PRESCOTT

HASTINGS

BAY CITY   MAIDEN ROCK

RED WING

WACOUTA
FRONTENAC
FLORENCE   STOCK-HOLM PEPIN

LAKE CITY

WABASHA   ALMA

KELLOGG

CHIPPEWA FALLS

EAU CLAIRE
(Ō-CLARE),
FRENCH FOR
"CLEAR WATER")

CHIPPEWA RIVER

DURAND

40

Minn suddenly awoke. PEOPLE? *HERE?* She fled in terror. . . . Another dam near Red Wing frightened her again. . . . *Then* came the "Sinker" of her "Hook-and-Line-River"!

Bottom-wise Minn was not bothered by waves — at first. But she did not like this lake-bed. Sometimes on solid rock, sometimes on bumpy boulders rolled down from the north, she could not sleep well! Town beaches held enough mud for a snooze, but she was shy. Big waves pried her loose, slapping her down like a teakettle lid at the boil! And what about these dizzy currents? She would lean on pushing water, but it slid out from under. She ached for a good stiff current going all one way. Blown off course at the surface time and again, washed shore to shore, dribbled along the bluffs — no wonder her built-in turtle patience wobbled under the strain.

Minn was not alone in her weariness. Little boats on Lake Pepin's calm can be dumped by sudden breezes. Shantyboats running downstream at its mercy are sometimes frightened. Big boats often call it black names. It *has* wrecked steamers!

Yet some creatures like Lake Pepin. Tourists lining boat-rails with cameras snap up its grandeur. Artists tear pants climbing the cliffs, for scenic paintings to sell for more paints and pants. Crows like Lake Pepin, too. They have fun fanning out from grassy heights on rising pillows of air, which lift them up in soaring spirals without batting a wing. And buzzards; crows and buzzards squat on the crags, spotting dead fish and boat-garbage miles up the lake, wondering if the trip would be worth it in all this wind. Yet these carefree creatures of the air are *above* Lake Pepin. Minn was *in* it. She could not soar away.

Almost every rock rearing from these majestic bluffs has its tale for telling. Folks just love the legend of the love-sick Indian Maid. . . . Right off them rocks she leaped — yes *sir!* Right over yonder! Smack-dab down she jumped — from any old height that comes handy for spinning the story. At times it seems that she soared out from altitudes higher than the mossy bluffs themselves. Sometimes 'twas for this reason, sometimes for that one — relatives somehow were mixed in it, see? . . . But on one point all tale-tellers agree — she aimed to get away from it all! And that part Minn might have understood. She, too, aimed to get away!

41

GREEN BAY
MACKINAC STRAITS
GEORGIAN BAY
FRENCH RIVER
LAKE NIPISSING
OTTAWA RIVER

ST. LAWRENCE RIVER
FLOWING TO THE SEA

MONTREAL

FRENCH FUR TRADE
FROM LAKE PEPIN AREA

LAKE SUPERIOR
PORTAGE
WISCONSIN RIVER
FOX RIVER
FORT SAINT ANTOINE
LAKE MICHIGAN
LAKE HURON
L. ERIE
L. ONTARIO
FORT
LAKE PEPIN
(ANTOINE IS AN-TWAN' IN FRENCH)
PORTAGE
PORTAGE
FORT
FORT

A "CASED" PELT, PULLED OFF LIKE A GLOVE—MARTEN, MINK, ETC.

A "PLEW" OR BEAVER SKIN DRIED OPEN "DRUM TIGHT"

PLEWS PRESSED INTO "BALE" FOR EASY PORTAGE

STRETCHERS

A GENTLEMAN'S "BEAVER HAT," 1670

BEAVER FUR ITSELF, REMOVED FROM THE SKIN, WAS IMPORTANT. IT WAS PRESSED INTO FELT FOR THE FINEST HATS.

"COUREUR DE BOIS," CANOEMAN, SCOUT, EXPLORER-DRESSED LIKE HIS INDIAN FRIENDS.

THE "VOYAGEUR" KEPT TO FRENCH COSTUME. HE WAS ALL-AROUND MAN OF CANOE TRAFFIC.

SMALL-RIVER CANOE
LARGE-RIVER CANOES
BIG-LAKE CANOE

On Lake Pepin's bottom, Minn found the wreck of a birch canoe. Clay had long preserved the canoe, but shifting currents had uncovered it. From far-off Montreal in French-Canada it had brought goods for the Indian fur trade at Fort St. Antoine, on Lake Pepin. It had weathered rapids and Great Lakes gales — only to sink within sight of the fort!

Minn waddled over small gunpowder kegs, bundles of guns and lead bars. Broken chests spilled copper bells into brass kettles. Knives and tomahawks were rusted in square chunks, their rawhide packs rotted away. Minn's feet sank in boxes of beads. She saw small glass discs that once were mirrors. Minn was now Captain and Crew of this cargo. Yet her voyage had ended two centuries and a half before she was born!

Minn's canoe had come here because of far-distant happenings. First, Spaniards had explored the South and the Gulf of Mexico, discovering the Lower Mississippi while searching for gold. Then Frenchmen came to the east coast, the Gulf of St. Lawrence; started the fur trade in Canada; and found the Upper Mississippi. In those early days the Mississippi, America's greatest south-flowing river, was first Spanish, then French. Its furry wealth from streams, forests and prairies went by canoe to the Great Lakes and their east-flowing outlet, St. Lawrence River — and on east to France.

Beaver skins were the main pelts of the fur trade, but Frenchmen traded for other pelts as well — sleek or woolly, striped, spotted or plain, besides buckskin and bison robes. Streams crawled with Indian canoes taking pelts to French forts, the frontier tradingposts, to be bound into bales for easy portaging. Minn's ancestors probably watched from the reeds as fur canoes sped to the Great Lakes and beyond; paddled and pushed and poled and portaged by chanting Frenchmen and Indians — known from forest campfires to castles in Europe as the gay "voyageur" (vwa'-ya-zhur', or "voyager"), and swift "coureur de bois" (koo'-rur'-duh-bwah', the "runner-of-the-woods").

For those who can listen, Lake Pepin's bluffs tell tales of the old voyageurs. Others hear only thunders, the roaring of wind and hissing of rain. Minn was hard of hearing. At last she found the way out of Lake Pepin — and rolled on down the River.

42

10. A COUNTRY OF BUILDERS

MINN was twelve when she fled Lake Pepin's bumps and churnings. But two more big dams made her feel much older. North of Winona she forgot her cares, wintering in mud.

Soon again came spring, walking upriver. Towboat tails spread wide and washed Minn out of bed. Floods raced, flipping her like so much foam — and flopped her over another dam without her realizing it. Floods tumbled her along their dappled miles. . . .

Towns drifted to Minn. Still sleepy, dazed and stiff in the cold flood waters, she scarcely could see the strange clusters of buildings barging into her vision. Towns sat at old steamboat landings in prim dignity; or drew back frayed skirts from the old-fashioned waterway to stare at railroads; or strode up the bluffs to watch shiny cars woosh by on a highway. Between towns, bare woodlands scrawled on the sky gray pencil scribblings. Meadows were smeared green crayon, plowed fields were brown chalk-rows, orchards were white-spattered bloom. How could Minn know that these woods and fields formed farms, school-districts, townships, counties and states with boundaries and names? Minn did not even know that anything had a name!

All these names have meaning. Some are Indian words, as they should be. For centuries Indians traveled the River, fished it, farmed its banks and left their names upon it. Then strange words came — French, Spanish, English, Scotch, Irish, German, Scandinavian; but the first strange words on the Upper River were French. . . .

French names still cling to the River's banks like beads on worn old buckskin; Trempealeau (trem'-pah-lo): La Crosse (lah-cross'); Prairie du Chien (doo-sheen'). Such names might not be at all real to Minn — but she *could* see beads. And below Prairie du Chien, bottom-walking at the mouth of the Wisconsin River, her aimless claws uncovered two tiny glass lumps in the silt. Curving her neck she stared solemnly down. No, that red eye and that white one belonged to no live creature. They meant nothing. . . . They meant nothing except that they had come here as gifts for possibly warlike Indians, and were lost from a canoe gliding to shore. For at this place white men had first gazed at the majesty of the Upper Mississippi.

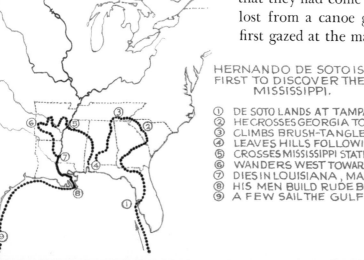

GREAT LAKES

HERNANDO DE SOTO IS
FIRST TO DISCOVER THE
MISSISSIPPI.

① DE SOTO LANDS AT TAMPA BAY, FLORIDA, JUNE 3, 1539.
② HE CROSSES GEORGIA TO SOUTH CAROLINA, NORTH CAROLINA.
③ CLIMBS BRUSH-TANGLED, FORESTED HILLS INTO TENNESSEE.
④ LEAVES HILLS FOLLOWING INDIANS TOWARD MOBILE, ALABAMA.
⑤ CROSSES MISSISSIPPI STATE, **DISCOVERS GREAT RIVER**, MAY 8, 1541.
⑥ WANDERS WEST TOWARD LITTLE ROCK, AND THROUGH ARKANSAS.
⑦ DIES IN LOUISIANA, MAY, 1542. IS BURIED IN THE GREAT RIVER.
⑧ HIS MEN BUILD RUDE BOATS, FLOAT DOWN TO THE RIVER'S MOUTH.
⑨ A FEW SAIL THE GULF AND REACH SPANISH TOWNS IN MEXICO.

44

① THE PRIEST AND THE WOODSMAN LEAVE ST. IGNACE, MICHIGAN, MAY 17, 1673.
② THESE FRIENDS PADDLE ACROSS LAKE MICHIGAN AND GREEN BAY.
③ UP FOX RIVER, THEY PORTAGE TO THE WISCONSIN RIVER.
④ THEY REACH THE MOUTH OF THE WISCONSIN RIVER.
⑤ **DISCOVER** THE UPPER MISSISSIPPI ON JUNE 17, 1673.
⑥ THEY PASS DE SOTO'S CROSSING (SOMEWHERE BELOW MEMPHIS).
⑦ THEY REACH THE ARKANSAS RIVER, AND TURN BACK NORTH.
⑧ THEY PADDLE UP THE ILLINOIS RIVER, THE DES PLAINES RIVER.
⑨ THEY PORTAGE TO CHICAGO RIVER AND REACH LAKE MICHIGAN.
⑩ UP LAKE MICHIGAN, THEY RETURN TO GREEN BAY IN SEPTEMBER, 1673.

A POINT OF DISCOVERY

The first people from Europe to see the *Lower* River had been Spanish soldiers. De Soto's army had landed in Florida, looping northward and west — an armor-scaled dragon snorting thunder and fire, seeking gold. De Soto found none — but he crossed the Lower River, died and was buried in it. His weary, wounded, returning army told Europe about the huge Mississippi. Yet for one hundred thirty-two years it was only a memory. No white man saw De Soto's discovery till Frenchmen found it again. . . .

The French settlers of Canada had long known the Great Lakes. But what lay to the west of them? The heads of the French government sent two men to find out. One, Père (Father) Marquette (mar-ket′) was an unselfish Jesuit missionary. The other, Louis Jolliet (zhol′-yay′), was expert in wilderness travel. At Green Bay on Lake Michigan, Indians warned Jolliet and Marquette that westward lay danger, and dangerous tribes. Yet in 1673 they left Green Bay, pushing west up Fox River, west down the Wisconsin. And one June day they saw a greater River before them, rolling south. The two canoes of the party went ashore. White men first stared at the vast Upper Mississippi. . . .

The River carried their dancing canoes far southward, yet they did not reach the Gulf of Mexico. At the Arkansas River, a little beyond where De Soto had crossed a century and a quarter before, they started back upstream. Working hard at their paddles they returned to the Illinois River, up that to the Des Plaines, the short Chicago and into Lake Michigan. Coasting north up the west shore, they returned to Green Bay. Jolliet and Marquette had made many Indian friends. Their canoes had traced the outline of an ancient flint point — a POINT OF DISCOVERY showing one way the French fur trade would later follow. . . .

Minn had nothing to do with Jolliet or Marquette nor with La Salle (lah-sal′) who, nine years after them, canoed clear to the Gulf and claimed the entire River for France. Minn's thoughts were only for egg laying. Each year she had hidden her eggs in forest mold, meadow soil or sandbar. Now, passing a soft-shelled turtle whose carapace fairly waved in the current, she made straight for the middle of a town!

LA SALLE'S "LOUISIANA" WAS ALL LAND DRAINED BY MISSISSIPPI R.

CANADA

MARQUETTE MADE HIS 3,000 MILE ROUND TRIP IN FOUR MONTHS. ROBERT DE LA SALLE TOOK ALMOST FOUR YEARS. MANY TIMES HE STARTED AND FAILED, BUT ALWAYS TRIED AGAIN.

① HE STARTS (NEAR BUFFALO) IN "GRIFFON" (FIRST SHIP BUILT OR SAILED ON GREAT LAKES), AUG 7, 1679.
② LANDING (ST. JOSEPH, MICH.), CANOES UP ST. JOSEPH RIVER TO SOUTH BEND, IND.
③ PORTAGES TO KANKAKEE RIVER, PADDLES INTO BIG ILLINOIS RIVER.
④ BUILDS FORT NEAR PEORIA, ILL. HIKES BACK TO CANADA IN DEEP SNOW.
⑤ HIS "GRIFFON" LOST, PORTAGES AT "TORONTO CARRYING PLACE" AUG., 1681.
⑥ AFTER MUCH BAD LUCK, PORTAGES OVER ICE AT CHICAGO, JAN. 1682.
⑦ AT LONG LAST ON THE MISSISSIPPI, BUILDS SMALL "FORT PRUDHOMME."
⑧ PROCLAIMS "LOUISIANA" FOR HIS FRENCH KING, LOUIS, APRIL 19, 1682.
⑨ RETURNS TO CANADA AND FRANCE, FOR SETTLERS TO COLONIZE LOUISIANA.
⑩ SAILING WITH SETTLERS, AIMS FOR THE MISSISSIPPI, BUT CAN'T FIND IT.
⑪ LANDS IN TEXAS. ONE MAN, ANGRY AT BEING LOST, MURDERS LA SALLE, 1687.

MINN PASSED A "SPINY SOFT-SHELLED TURTLE".

"EFFIGY" MOUNDS (EF'-FY-JY) FORM SHAPES OF ANIMALS, BIRDS, REPTILES, PEOPLE AND NAMELESS THINGS. THEY MAY HAVE BEEN SHRINES TO ANIMAL SPIRITS.

TODAY MANY TRIBES TREAT THE TURTLE AS A SACRED INDIVIDUAL. TURTLES PLAY IMPORTANT ROLES IN THE LEGENDS AND CEREMONIES OF MANY PEOPLES. FROM THE MANY TURTLE EFFIGY MOUNDS LEFT IN AMERICA, WE CAN GUESS THAT THE TURTLE (AND PROBABLY A SNAPPING TURTLE, AT THAT) WAS A VERY IMPORTANT FELLOW!

THE MOUND BUILDERS WERE FINE ARTISTS AND EXPERT CRAFTSMEN. HERE ARE A FEW OF THE MANY MATERIALS SHAPED BY THEIR CRUDE TOOLS.

STONE "PLATFORM PIPES" NEED NO PIPE-STEMS.

CLAY POTS BY THE TON ARE FOUND.

WHITE QUARTZ
BLACK OBSIDIAN
MICA (ISINGLASS)

COPPER FROM LAKE SUPERIOR COUNTRY MADE TOOLS AND ORNAMENTS. BY MUCH POUNDING COPPER IS HARDENED, BUT CANNOT BE "TEMPERED."

CLAM-SHELL FOR TOOLS AND ORNAMENTS. PEARLS FROM THE CLAM HAVE BEEN FOUND BY THE THOUSANDS. READ "THE MOUND BUILDERS" BY HENRY CLYDE CHETRONE, EXPERT ON MOUNDS. (HE TAUGHT THIS AUTHOR TO FLAKE FLINT.)

Minn dug her nest on a riverbank among neatly made, shed-sized hills with trees growing on them. A busy, prosperous town had stood here, but not even early Frenchmen had seen its bark buildings. All town dwellings had fallen to dust before white men came, leaving only the hills to tell of those ghostly "Mound Builders".

Tribes of these ancient Indians built thousands of hill-mounds across America — especially up the Mississippi and its tributaries. Some mounds are still gigantic monuments heaped over honored dead. Steep pyramids, once topped by log-timbered temples, look down on terraces where chiefs once lived. Fort walls wander through woodlands, humped in ridges under the sod like workings of giant moles. Long, wide creatures, built of rounded earth, sprawl patiently across pastures. They are reptiles, grown over with weeds; grass-furred beasts; brush-feathered birds stretching earthen wings — waiting for magic of altar-smoke to give them life. . . .

How were these mounds in America made? By babies lifting fistfuls of sand; by boys and girls, women and men digging with clam-shells and deer-bone shovels. After the fishing, the hunt and cornfield duties, endless rows of people with baskets trudged uphill, carrying gifts of soil to a hungry, growing mound. . . . The day would come when strange, pale-faced farmers would build white houses on some mounds, and bright red barns; other sacred mounds would be leveled to make way for towns. . . .

The ancient Mound Builders, gone for centuries, might not be real to Minn — but now they caused her no end of trouble. In hastily digging her nest she came to many hard lumps. She clawed out obsidian arrowheads, bits of clay pottery, a carved-stone pipe. And finally, after several heaves, she kicked up an axe-head of solid coppr. For such treasures any museum collector might have given Minn a private pool, fresh meat for a lifetime, unlimited rest and quiet. Minn was interested only in digging her nest in a hurry. At least three dozen eggs were packed in a mixture of soil and some two hundred pearl beads. . . . Kicking dirt over everything, Minn waddled back to the water. In her own way, she had dug and built her own mound. . . .

46

11. RIVER LIFE HAS ITS DOWNS AND UPS

MINN left her eggs packed in ancient pearls, and lazily drifted away from the mouth of the Wisconsin River. When she scrambled along the Mississippi's east bank, she wandered in Wisconsin. At times she swam over to snooze in Iowa. But both banks often roared with towns. Every five or ten miles, every month or so, a new town noisy with people floated by on purpose to insult Minn! Humans were so terrifying! And yet, simplest things might frighten them. A barefooted boy cornered Minn near shore, aiming a fish-spear at her. Before throwing the spear he stepped on a silt-covered bump and splashed away, howling in high vibrations. Minn explored that bump in the sand. What had scared that boy? She found only a jagged, broken bottle.

The River's deep channel often thundered with towboats pushing long barges. Churning screws and paddle-wheels sent many a shudder through sensitive creatures. Minn kept midway between such boat-channels and banks where people might be. Here stretched a peaceful, shimmering world of leafy islands and weed-swirling, sunken mud-bars. Here kingfishers speared fish, plunging down like blue stones falling out of the sky. Snaky-necked cormorants perched upright on snags, or chased fish. With a blur of webbed feet and quick-beating wings they "flew" under water, past Minn.

Birds were certainly puzzling creatures. Most ducks, for example, nested in marshes; but bright-colored wood ducks nested in holes in trees. One day near an island, sleepy Minn saw a wood duck, half out of her tree-hole. The duck peered up and down, but did not seem to notice Minn's stick-like head. After the duck flew down to the bank, twelve fuzzy, fat marbles sprang from the nest. One by one they popped out of the hole, dropped fifteen feet, bounced on hard ground, and rolled. Some minutes later, Minn was fully awake. Those balls were *tasty young ducklings!* Tightly huddled together into a plate-sized, downy raft, they were swimming upstream after their mother! Slow Minn could not overtake them. . . . It was curious how twelve birds, never knowing the outside world, could suddenly leap from a hollow nest, bounce on hard earth, swim to another island and disappear in weeds — all in ten minutes!

48

THE KINGFISHER TUNNELS INTO A RIVER BANK TO NEST.

THE DOUBLE-CRESTED CORMORANT NESTS IN COLONIES ON BARE ROCKS OR IN HIGH TREES IN SWAMPS.

(A FINE, LARGE BOOK ON BIRDS: "NATURAL HISTORY OF THE BIRDS OF EASTERN AND CENTRAL NORTH AMERICA" BY MR. FORBUSH AND MR. MAY. ROGER TORY PETERSON DRAWS BIRDS FOR QUICK IDENTIFICATION IN HIS "EASTERN" AND "WESTERN" GUIDE BOOKS. A PETERSON FIELD GUIDE TO THE BIRDS IS A HANDY HIKING COMPANION.

WOOD DUCKS PERCH IN TREES AND NEST IN HOLES.

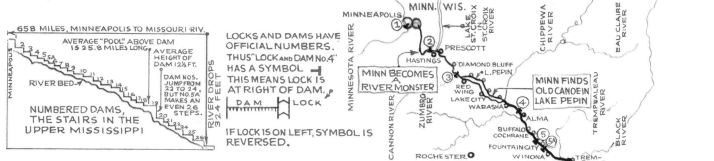

Ten times, since Minneapolis, Minn had been frightened by dams! It was all very monotonous. From upriver, each dam looked like a bridge across a quiet lake. Minn would drift toward it. Without warning she might be hurled over, as at the Water-Wall; or sucked under and down with sticks and boulders, shot through an opening, banged and walloped by water!

From the Minneapolis Water-Wall to the Missouri River, Old Mississip drops three hundred twenty-four feet. In one sheer drop, this would make one waterfall like four stacked-up Niagara Falls. But all this water does not drop in one place. It runs quietly flat, or it boils in rapids, for some six hundred sixty miles. The River was once risky for steamboats, between the "Saints" — St. Louis and St. Paul. Special pilots lived near certain rapids to steer the boats through. So many steamboats went aground that warehouses sprang up to shelter wrecked cargoes, and towns grew around them. But today, twenty-six dams between Minneapolis and the Missouri River have made the roaring Mississippi into a peaceful stairway. To climb upstairs or down, concrete "locks" at each dam raise or lower all boats, big and little, another step in the River.

Minn disliked dams even more than people. She flopped over some, suffered through others, and cheated a few — such as Dam Number 10 at Guttenberg, Iowa. On an island she walked over a built-up bank or "levee" (lev'-ee) — and found the dam was behind her! But Dam Number 11, at Eagle Point, snatched Minn. She hugged her shell, helpless as a kernel of Iowa corn in a mill. Though not ground to bits, Minn was dizzy. She drifted three miles into the city of Dubuque, banging submerged wing-dams on the way, without knowing it. When her senses returned, she decided against dams! Though she might have to climb bluffs to escape this DUG-DITCH-RIVER valley, she was going away! She charged to the east bank — and limped into Illinois. Somewhere, up on the prairie, would be a peaceful pond. The River and its works could hammer her no more!

However, Minn met a highway; and honking, hissing monsters. Spinning tires straddled her, flipped her over, ran across the dragging edge of her carapace where, luckily, she had no leg to be crushed. After that, she gave up and hurried back to her Mississippi.

49

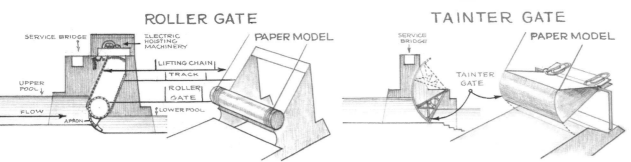

SERVICE BRIDGE
ELECTRIC HOISTING MACHINERY
PAPER MODEL

LIFTING CHAIN
TRACK
ROLLER GATE

UPPER POOL

FLOW
APRON
LOWER POOL

SERVICE BRIDGE
PAPER MODEL
TAINTER GATE

AN UPPER MISSISSIPPI DAM

TAINTER GATES
ROLLER GATES

THE "POOL" ABOVE DAM
DIRECTION OF CURRENT
LOCK
GATES
GATES

GUIDE WALL FOR SLIDING BARGES INTO THE LOCKS

Minn never could like going violently through underwater gates of dams But, now thirteen, she no longer fled blindly from people, and their fishhooks worked for her. Under rows of shantyboats moored among islands, she was sure to find fishlines sagging down from the surface. When a lazy catfish gulped bait on bottom, Minn waddled eagerly over. One snap killed it and, holding it down with her front feet, she ate. She stopped promptly when she came near the hooks inside. Too often lines were hauled up with only fish-heads dangling. *Then* things happened! While Minn rolled off like a thrown-away plate, shantyboat people vainly probed the mud for a "thievin' turtle"! Poles, oars and spears jabbed holes along bottom like sewing machines gone wild.

Always hungry, Minn began to grow careless. She trailed a hooked catfish into a rusty lard can. Pushing past dents, she was suddenly stuck! The lively fish flopped beneath her. Then the stout line jerked, and pulled up the tin and two captives.

"I grannies! Marthy, look here! Breakfast comes ready-canned, this mornin'!"

"*Cat*fish again!" snorted Martha. "Luke, it's a wonder we don't grow catfish faces, we eat so many! Hm. . . . A three-legged she-turtle. Reckon I don't feel like dressin' turtle meat right now. Pop 'er in th' swill-bar'l to fatten up some!"

Thus, near Galena Junction, Illinois, Minn began riding in a barrel. It stood at the stern of a shantyboat, near an old outboard motor and a coop full of cackling hens. Three yellow cats watched as Martha said, " 'Scuse me, Miss Turtle," pushing Minn under skim milk and table scraps with a big dipper. The dipper came up brimming with dainties, while Minn arose under it, hissing and clawing wildly at the barrel's slippery walls. But Martha continued in soothing tones, "It's this way, Miss Turtle. I mix this swill with grain mash, fer th' hen-trough. So, you see, we git fresh eggs from these leftovers. No waste. An' you'll git to like that bar'l, I reckon. We eat good, an' so will you. Luke, he hauls cans of skim milk on his wheelbarrow — from some farm or dairy near where we might be stoppin'. You'll float easy in a whole bar'l of food, an' git fat as a pig, an' then ——" But Martha did not finish.

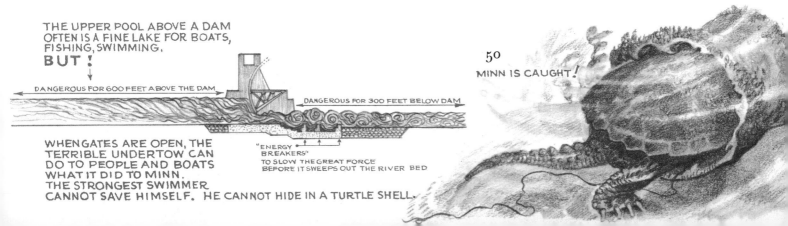

THE UPPER POOL ABOVE A DAM OFTEN IS A FINE LAKE FOR BOATS, FISHING, SWIMMING.
BUT!

DANGEROUS FOR 600 FEET ABOVE THE DAM

DANGEROUS FOR 300 FEET BELOW DAM

WHEN GATES ARE OPEN, THE TERRIBLE UNDERTOW CAN DO TO PEOPLE AND BOATS WHAT IT DID TO MINN. THE STRONGEST SWIMMER CANNOT SAVE HIMSELF. HE CANNOT HIDE IN A TURTLE SHELL.

"ENERGY BREAKERS" TO SLOW THE GREAT FORCE BEFORE IT SWEEPS OUT THE RIVER BED

50
MINN IS CAUGHT!

12. RIDE THE RIVER IN A BARREL

RIDING the River in a barrel was fun — till the shantyboat came to the next dam. Up through boat-timbers, up through the barrel, Minn felt its shuddering roar. She raced around in her prison. The cats sat on the coop to watch her. Martha came.

"Luke, has she eaten too much? Could she be sick?" . . . Listen, Miss Turtle. No need fer frettin'. We're comin' to Belleview, Ioway, an' Dam Number 12. . . . Luke, that's *it!* She's skeered of dams! . . . Hush, Miss Turtle! This'un won't hurt you. Them concrete walls, both sides of us — we're floatin' into a lock. . . . Now solid steel gates are closin' behind us. . . . Now th' water's sinkin' — runnin' out under th' front gates, an' our boat settles down, down — easy-like, no fuss at all. . . . Front gates are openin' — we're movin' out — see, there's th' River again. . . . Miss Turtle, you jest took a twelve-foot step down that river-stair. . . . Luke, now she's plumb calm. . . ."

Minn was less frightened at Dam 13, above Clinton, Iowa. At Dam 14, in quiet country near Pleasant Valley, she scarcely stirred. But Dam 15 lay nestled among big vibrations — busy Moline and Rock Island to the east, Davenport to the west, rapids roaring between, the locks "spang against Arsenal Island", as Martha said. "That's why, Luke, Miss Turtle's in a tizzy again!" But Luke was too busy to answer.

"Maybe, Miss Turtle", continued Martha, "you got a good right to be restless here. Many a battle was brewed hereabouts; Injuns killin' Injuns, killin' whites, whites killin' Injuns — like they was all playin' a game. Yep, this very island once saw a British fort built; then a frontier American fort. An' it has been an arsenal — a place fer makin' and storin' huge supplies fer armies — for many wars. Ever hear of th' Civil War? Two of my great grand-dads fought each other in it — one fer th' North, one fer th' South. Both died of lead bullets — molded, maybe, right over yonder. Th' slaves got freed; th' South got plumb ruined; an' th' War goes on to this day at supper tables along this River. But if folks could of talked it all over *first* ——"

"Marthy!" yelled Luke. "*Stop* talkin'! Git up front an' steer! Motor's actin' up again! Big boats are crowdin' us! We might git *sunk* while you gab to a *turtle!*"

TWO BOATS MEET.
THE BOAT IN THE
RIGHT-HAND LOCK
IS BOUND UPSTREAM.

52

Minn "took it plumb easy, after Rock Island." She did not hate anything now. She liked Martha, and would surface at her whistle, taking fish or meat held down to her. Martha often let her exercise in a canvas chicken-pen on deck while she cleaned out the swill-barrel.

At grassy old landings where planks linked shantyboats to paths, Luke brought new-found friends to the "porch" to "set a spell" and hear him tell how — "with timbers from three wrecked steamboats, I built this EVANGELINE NUMBER TWO. 'Evangeline' comes from Longfellow's poem, which Marthy can recite whole ropes of. Passin' noisy factories, she'll sing out '*This* is th' *for*est pri-*mee*-vul, th' *mur*murin' *pines* an' th' *hem*locks!' It's all about French folks from Canada. Long ago, what with politics an' wars, French families got run out of Acadia, up in Nova Scotia. Them Acadians went down th' Mississippi an' th' Atlantic coast, to settle along th' Gulf. Descendants are still called 'Cajuns' — short fer Acadians. Sad, her life was — Evangeline's. Marthy named this boat fer her."

All that summer the EVANGELINE II floated lazily south. At Hamburg, Illinois, Luke explained river charts to three boys. He was saying "Yep, this is our second trip. Minneapolis to New Orleans, we sold th' first EVANGELINE, went back by train, an' built this 'un better. We had worked hard at farmin' — laid a little money by — felt we'd like to grow old, easy-like, on th' Mississippi. . . . See th' chart — Wisconsin River — that's where Pere Marquette first saw this stream. An' round th' bend below your Hamburg is where him an' his pal, Jolliet, headed fer th' Great Lakes up th' Illinois. . . . Back near Dubuque, here, we picked up th' turtle, ready-canned, as I said. An' after Rock Island come Muscatine, th' Ioway River, Big Burlington — an' little Nauvoo, th' old Mormon town — Keokuk at Des Moines River, end of Ioway — Quincy, Illinois — Hannibal, Missouri ——"

"Mark Twain's town!" cried a boy, the others adding "He wrote about Tom Sawyer an' Huck Finn!" — "He was a steamboat pilot!" — "He could slide a steamboat over a bar by breathin' out quick an' hoistin' his pants, I betcha!" — "He sure knew th' River!"

"Yes," said Martha, passing by. "An' through his pen slid words to make th' whole world know our river. . . . For him, lonely words linked arms an' sang across th' page."

SPREAD THE MISSISSIPPI'S BANKS APART, AND A FRENCH VOYAGEUR (WITH A MINNESOTA PEAKED CAP, AN IOWA FACE, MISSOURI BEARD) TALKS TO AN ILLINOIS TRIBESMAN IN A WISCONSIN TURBAN WITH UPPER-MICHIGAN TOP.

"Yes, Missus Martha," said one boy, "we know about Mark Twain." Another added quickly, "An' we know *all* about *turtles,* too! They live for five hundred years, an' if they bite you they keep a holt till either it thunders or th' sun goes down!"

"That sure would be bad!" said Martha. "Imagine me steerin' EVANGELINE TWO through river traffic — Miss Turtle swingin' from my elbow like a ball an' chain, all tuckered out, not able to let go till sundown! . . . But snappers do strike hard, an' hold on long enough, anyhow, to start such stories about sundown an' thunder. As fer age — I read about a tortoise livin' to almost two hundred. But snappers are old at forty."

"Jest goes to show," said Luke, "how worry an' bad temper can kill you young!"

After an hour or so of turtle talk, the boys had to leave. Waving good-bye, they disappeared in sunflowers. One voice returned — "An' *you* said we knew *all* about turtles!"

Next day, with motor trouble, EVANGELINE II headed for the mouth of the Illinois, forty miles south of Hamburg. She met a "tow" — a raft of barges pushed by a towboat — as long as an ocean liner, and as difficult to steer. The sweating Pilot tried to miss a shantyboat, rowed wildly by a woman. But EVANGELINE II was bumped!

From the towboat came the Captain's voice by "bull-horn." This loudspeaker "roared fit to wake th' dead," as Luke told it afterward. "Yep, an' he bellered out 'LISTEN, UNCLE!' As if I could *keep* from listenin' with both ears plugged! 'US BIG BOATS CAN'T TURN OUT FER EVERY FLOATIN' CHIP!' An' Marthy yelled back loud enough to split oak planks, but he couldn't hear. 'Twas Marthy a-screechin' an' th' bull-horn a-bawlin' till we drifted astern to th' towboat an' clumb up on her deck."

"Yes," Martha would continue primly, "an' I gave that cap'n a piece of my mind, I certainly did! But he turned out to be a gentleman. Invited us to dinner. Gave us *twenty dollars* — said 'twas fer scrapin' our paint, though Luke bought enough paint later fer *fifty cents!* His cook filled our tipped-over bar'l with garbage from his galley. But all of us, includin' that nice cap'n, was sad that Miss Turtle slid spang out th' bar'l an' overboard when we bumped. But — well, maybe she's happier back in her river. . . ."

54

CLARKS-
VILLE
MISSISSIPPI
RIVER
HAMBURG
ILLINOIS
RIVER
WINFIELD
CAP AU GRIS
GRAFTON
LAST LOCK
AND DAM
ALTON
MISSOURI R.
(MISS-OU-RI
MEANS "BIG
MUDDY" IN
INDIAN.)
ST.
LOUIS
EAST
ST. LOUIS
MERAMEC R.
MISSISSIPPI R.

FROM HIS CANOE
MARQUETTE SAW
INDIAN PAINTINGS
OF MONSTERS ON
THE ALTON CLIFFS.
UNTIL THE ROCKS
WERE QUARRIED
AWAY FOR HOUSES
IN 1846-47, INDIANS
PASSING BY MADE
GIFTS OF TOBACCO
TO THE "PIASA BIRD".

LANDSCAPE WITH
BLUFFS AT ALTON, ILL.
RE-DRAWN FROM OLD
PRINT RE-PUBLISHED
BY CITY ART MUSEUM
OF ST. LOUIS IN ITS
BOOK, "MISSISSIPPI
PANORAMA."
THE PIASA FIGURE DOES
NOT FOLLOW THE PRINT,
BUT HAS BEEN DRAWN BY
AUTHOR FROM TRANSLATIONS
OF MARQUETTE'S ACCOUNT.

13. SENTINELS OF THE CROSSROADS

MINN was once more in water. After sloshing in skim milk all summer, she found this water-stuff quite thin! She swam, yet her nose didn't bump barrel staves. No more did she scramble in circles. But she was so fat! She tired easily. She stopped.

Then she was hungry. Her eyes peered blankly. No food. No chunks of tomatoes, cabbage, chicken, pork fat, trimmings of beef. No fish-heads! Not even a smell! Minn sank at the thought — to the bottom. Then she remembered. Snuggling herself into the mud, she let it bury her. Only her mouth was above it, wide open. Her smooth tongue wiggled like a fat worm, and a fish dived at it. Minn was eating again!

Minn gave in to the River. She went along. She saw bluffs, as at old Lake Pepin. Marquette had seen an Indian monster painted on these rocks — but Minn knew only about the rocks; a wind slammed her against them. She fought back to safe, deep channel.

Alton, Illinois, came toward her with noise and confusion, but vibrations no longer bothered her. THEN it happened! *Minn rolled and churned through another dam!* This was Minn's *last* dam. Though more dams would be built on the River, this was Minn's last step down the Upper Mississippi stairs. She did not know this. She was in a daze for eight more miles. She did not notice new silt in her river.

Minn's northern river was being joined by a western river of plains and Rocky Mountains. It smelled of cottonwood, willow, buffalo-grass and sage — but the main smell was *mud*. "Big Muddy," the wild Missouri, was teaming up with Ole Mississip — yet each was cautious. Green waters hugged the east bank, yellow waters held to the west, with Minn swimming in and out between colored strands. In another mile the currents and colors mingled. Minn's River turned golden-brown.

Fat Minn was only a small bead between two-colored cords as the thick side-line from the west was spliced to the main Hook-and-Line. Here the green, northern Upper Mississippi ended. For the next two hundred miles, Minn would travel a wider, muddy, double-thick line — the Middle Mississippi. Then the broad Ohio River would add its eastern line — and a braided, triple-strand Lower Mississippi would flow to the Gulf.

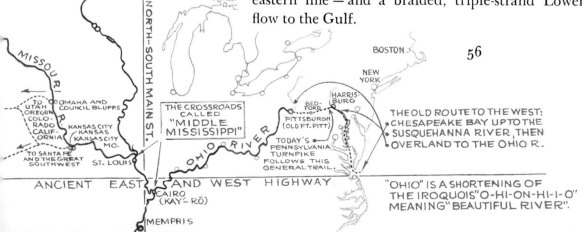

MISSOURI
TO
UTAH
OREGON
COLO-
RADO
CALIF-
ORNIA
OMAHA AND
COUNCIL BLUFFS
KANSAS CITY
KANSAS
KANSAS CITY
MO.
TO SANTA FE
AND THE GREAT
SOUTHWEST
ST. LOUIS
NORTH-SOUTH MAIN ST.
THE CROSSROADS
CALLED
"MIDDLE
MISSISSIPPI"
OHIO RIVER
TODAY'S
PENNSYLVANIA
TURNPIKE
FOLLOWS THIS
GENERAL TRAIL.
BED-
FORD
PITTSBURGH
(OLD FT. PITT)
HARRIS-
BURG
BOSTON
NEW
YORK
THE OLD ROUTE TO THE WEST:
CHESAPEAKE BAY UP TO THE
SUSQUEHANNA RIVER, THEN
OVERLAND TO THE OHIO R.
ANCIENT EAST AND WEST HIGHWAY
CAIRO
(KAY-RŌ)
MEMPHIS
"OHIO" IS A SHORTENING OF
THE IROQUOIS "O-HI-ON-HI-I-O"
MEANING "BEAUTIFUL RIVER".

The Middle Mississippi scrawls a letter Z — with St. Louis, Missouri, at the top and Cairo (kay'-ro), Illinois, at the bottom. This Z marks a crossroads — the crossing place of two giant water-highways. Countless people have traveled west from the east coast — starting by boat, then walking over Appalachian ranges, then drifting down the Ohio, paddling up the Middle Mississippi, pushing west up the Missouri. Indians, trappers, traders, miners and settlers have followed this trail — the great east-west water-trail crossing the great north-south water-trail at the Middle Mississippi.

Ancient Mound Builders once lived at this crossroads. Along the Middle Mississippi they heaped their monuments — some of them quite huge, such as the Cahokia Mounds near East St. Louis. Like those ancient hill-shapers, the soil-cutting rivers leave mounds — shapes of animals, birds, oddly crumpled outlines of mysterious beings — magic Sentinels-of-Crossroads.

The Middle Mississippi has carved itself into a magic River-Bear, balanced on his nose. St. Louis and other cities surround the heel of his rear foot. The city of Cairo clings to the fur of his lower jaw. The Ohio gives him front legs, an old lake forms his eye, while his round ear is tipped by Cape Girardeau (ji-rar'-doh to natives).

Minn left the Missouri, following the Bear's rear foot some fifteen miles to the middle of St. Louis. She clung to flat stones paving the waterfront. She sensed a haze of tall buildings at the top of the long slope. A far-off Negro boy walked toward her, along this bank where a river-town had grown into a huge city. It had seen the fur trade. It had seen the start of the Santa Fe Trail to the southwest; Lewis and Clark setting out to explore the unknown northwest; Mormons going to Utah; Settlers moving in covered wagons to Oregon; gold-seekers bound for California or Colorado. . . .

Minn saw only the Negro boy, larger now. No ghosts stood beside her — no Indians, Frenchmen, Spaniards, Mountain-Men in buckskins; no blue-clad soldiers, red-shirted miners; no buffalo hunters, stage-drivers, cowboys, Irish layers of railroad track. No forests of steamboat stacks crowded these stones. Towboats roared by, doing the work of old-time steamboats. Nobody came but the Negro boy, thinking of turtle soup. Minn left.

57

THE EADS BRIDGE, ST. LOUIS
(FROM AN OLD ENGRAVING)

"PANORAMAS" OF THE MISSISSIPPI WERE FAMOUS. ONE WAS "FOUR HUNDRED YARDS", ONE FOUR MILES LONG." SIX DIFFERENT PAINTERS, WITH HELPERS, PAINTED PANORAMAS IN ST. LOUIS SAIL-LOFTS DURING 1840 TO 1850. THE MOST FAMOUS WAS HENRY LEWIS, ENGLISHMAN (SEE PAGE 33, FORT SNELLING). JUST BELOW THE WATER-WALL HE BUILT PLANKS ACROSS TWO CANOES-PITCHED HIS TENT ON THIS, DRIFTED DOWN, SKETCHING, AND PAINTED THE RESULTS FOR HIS "MOVING PICTURE."

(FOR MORE ON THIS SUBJECT READ "UPPER MISSISSIPPI" BY WALTER HAVIGHURST. ALSO "MISSISSIPPI PANORAMA" MENTIONED ON PAGE 56 OF THIS BOOK.)

The Middle Mississippi held much magic. There was the Eads Bridge, of iron, dating from after Civil War days. Folks once said "That self-taught Eads boy — he thinks he can do things engineers have never dared!" But his "wild scheme" for raising sunken cargoes brought him a fortune. His "Eads Jetties" made the River clean its own muddy mouth. Now Minn, in St. Louis, drifted under soaring iron of his dream-bridge.

A century ago there was other magic, too. Artists drifted down the River, making sketches. At St. Louis they painted long "panoramas" from their drawings — rolls of painted cloth to be slowly unwound before audiences. Thus bright colors — ground-up silts of earths and minerals, mixed with oils — were smeared on cotton cloth and shown in cities of America and Europe. Countless people who would never see the River itself watched its magic roll past as though they gazed from the decks of a river steamboat.

For three years Minn left *her* yearly magic gift along the Middle Mississippi, laying her eggs in sun-warmed soil. At one wooded old island, a troop of painted terrapin watched as she came ashore to nest near a blown-up steamboat. Over five thousand such steamboats have been wrecked on the Middle River alone. This shifty river-character also robbed Illinois of land to bribe Missouri with it — or the other way around. The town of St. Genevieve, once on the bank, now sat inland. Near-by St. Mary's, cut off from the River, now lay four miles from the main channel. Minn walked on silted stones which once had been part of Kaskaskia, important French frontier town.

Opposite Grand Tower, on the River-Bear's shoulder, Minn passed a towering rock. Long streaks across it marked the sinking levels of an ancient, inland sea. Minn passed Cape Girardeau, famous old River city on a hill of the Bear's ear. But at the Bear's eyebrow, Minn's thousand-mile-long, DUG-DITCH-RIVER ended. As an old-timer might say, "Right here at Commerce, Missouri, Paul Bunyan quit plowin' th' giant furrow, an' him an' his blue ox, Babe, lit out fer Bemidji an' th' North Woods again!" Walls of the ditch were dwindling away. From here to the Gulf, man-made levees would take the place of bluffs along the western banks. The magic River-Bear stared down at a new kind of river.

58

GRAFTON
ALTON
MISSOURI R.
ST. LOUIS WAS ONCE "MOUND CITY"
CAHOKIA MOUNDS
E. ST. LOUIS
KASKASKIA R.
HERCULANEUM
HUNDREDS OF ANCIENT MOUNDS DOT THIS WHOLE "MIDDLE RIVER."
FESTUS CRYSTAL CITY
SAINT GENEVIEVE
ST. MARY'S
BIG MUDDY (NOT TO BE CONFUSED WITH THE MISSOURI!)
WABASH RIVER
SHAWNEE TOWN
GRAND TOWER
ELIZABETH TOWN
ILLINOIS
OHIO R.
GOLCONDA
CAPE GIRARDEAU
A HALF-WAY PLACE FOR MINN AND THE MISSISSIPPI WITH OVER A THOUSAND MILES STRETCHING NORTH AND SOUTH. "DUG-DITCH-RIVER" ENDS HERE, "BUILT-UP-RIVER" BEGINS. BELOW CAIRO, IT RUNS HIGHER THAN THE RICH, SILTED LAND IT CROSSES.
THEBES
COMMERCE
MOUNDS
SMITH-LAND
CUMBERLAND R.
MOUND CITY
PADUCAH
TENNESSEE R.
CAIRO
MISSOURI
KENTUCKY

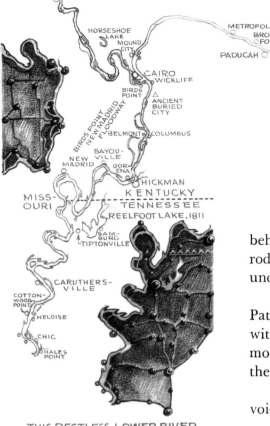

THIS RESTLESS LOWER RIVER CARVES FANTASTIC MASKS IN ITS DARK SOIL, SOMETHING LIKE THE MASKS CARVED BY ANCIENT INDIANS. TOWNS ARE SET IN THE MASKS AS THE MOUND BUILDERS SET PEARLS. IF YOU KNOW OF THESE TOWNS, YOU MAY FIND THEM BY FOLLOWING LINES, WHICH ARE ROADS.

14. WHEN WATER RUNS OVER LAWNS AND THINGS

MINN passed Cairo in the night. She saw only the glow of it behind high flood-walls. She met the Ohio and, in its added current, rode thirty-two miles to Hickman, Kentucky. Beside Hickman's hill, under a boat, she snoozed in a storm of sinking, drifting silt.

On the landing above Minn a woman was saying "Bill, meet Patricia, and her cousin, Linda. They're from Michigan, driving south with friends. They have studied about the Mississippi, but saw it this morning for the first time. You're an Army Engineer — please explain the River for them. Good-bye, girls — I'll pick you up in an hour."

"How do you do, Miss Patricia, and Miss Linda," boomed Bill's voice. "Sit right down! I hope you like our big old river?"

"It's big, but awfully muddy! And *all* its *names* ——"

"Yes, Linda and I have been hearing 'Upper,' 'Lower,' 'Middle Mississippi.' We can't seem to get them all straight."

"If you got them *straight,* they surely *wouldn't* be right!" The Engineer's voice chuckled. "This whole river is more downright crooked than a cottonmouth snake, and sometimes more poisonous! We divide the River into sections, to tell which part we're talking about. Different groups of engineers oversee each part. But another reason is just simple geology. The *Upper* Mississippi *made* the *Lower.* Understand?"

"Yes," said Patricia. "But do *you* understand, Linda?" and Linda said, "Nope!"

"It's this way, Miss Linda," said Bill. "Here's a map. Now, the Upper River — from Lake Itasca down, dug soil from the earth. Together with the Middle River, it spread that soil for the Lower River to run on. Like laying down a bed of sand for a railroad track. Yes, that's it! A great big track-bed south to the Gulf of Mexico!"

"I know about railroad tracks," said Linda. "But rivers ——"

"See here. Did you girls ever forget and leave a hose, running full, on a lawn?"

"*I* did!" said Linda. "And *was* I *spanked* — uh — *rep*-rimanded! I put bricks to hold the end down, and Pat called to me, and I forgot the faucet. *What* a *ditch!*"

60

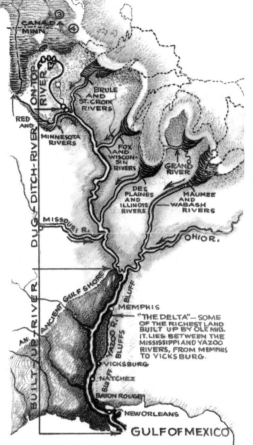

"GOOD!" cried Bill. "I mean – it certainly was regrettable that you required reprimanding, but – where did all that dirt go? It washed out – it went *somewhere* ——"

"Did it!" squealed Linda. "Down the drive, down the street past Rosemary's, like a big muddy fan spread out, all wiggly with water! It dried hard. Cars bumped on it!"

"That's exactly what happened, right here!" said Bill. "Linda, your hose (that's the River) gouged a ditch in the lawn (the Upper Mississippi's ditch) and spread that soil in a fan down the street (which used to be a long, thin arm of the Gulf of Mexico, reaching to north of Cairo). Look away over there – at all that flat land. Clear to the present Gulf, south of New Orleans – hundreds of miles of it – all was built up by gouging rivers, in just that way. This River, and other streams, still flow through that mud – rains keep the faucet running. But long ago, a GIANT HYDRANT was wide open!"

"I'd like to see *that!*" said Linda. "What's a Giant Hydrant?"

"It was a glacier – a blanket of ice across Canada, thick as a sky-scraper is tall. Sun began to melt the ice, turning on the Giant Hydrant. Ice-water made our Great Lakes run over. It also spread out in a huge puddle, called 'Lake Agassiz.' Unmelted walls of the glacier kept the waters from running northward or east. When hot sun turned the Giant Hydrant on full, torrents of water gushed south through the 'hose' of the Mississippi (already lying there), gouging a 'ditch' through a thousand miles of lawn.' "

"*Then* what?" cried Linda. "How was it turned off?"

"When the entire glacier melted, Great Lakes currents ran east, as they still do. Lake Agassiz drained north, and ran dry. Today, Indians up there wonder about beaches winding through dry woods. Deepest parts of the old puddle still hold rainwater, such as Lake Winnipeg and smaller lakes, dotting the ancient bed. The Giant Hydrant was turned off, but soil it had gouged out filled up a long, thin Gulf."

"It's hard to imagine the Gulf away up here," said Patricia.

"It does take imagination," agreed Bill. "Think of it – salty waves washing northward, to above Cairo. But the River filled it with sand and clay, pushing the salt waves back. If you were a turtle, you'd see how this could happen. Linda, can you be a turtle?"

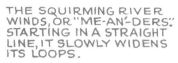
THE SQUIRMING RIVER
WINDS, OR "ME-AN'-DERS."
STARTING IN A STRAIGHT
LINE, IT SLOWLY WIDENS
ITS LOOPS.

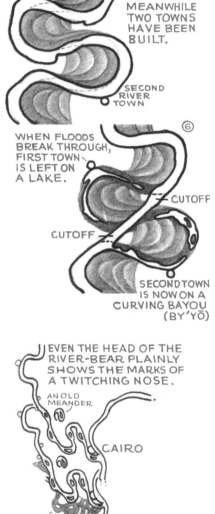

① ② ③ ④

⑤

FIRST
RIVER
TOWN

AT LAST THE
MEANDERS
ARE ABOUT
TO BREAK.
MEANWHILE
TWO TOWNS
HAVE BEEN
BUILT.

SECOND
RIVER
TOWN

WHEN FLOODS
BREAK THROUGH,
FIRST TOWN
IS LEFT ON
A LAKE.

⑥

CUTOFF

CUTOFF

SECOND TOWN
IS NOW ON A
CURVING BAYOU
(BY'YŌ)

EVEN THE HEAD OF THE
RIVER-BEAR PLAINLY
SHOWS THE MARKS OF
A TWITCHING NOSE.

AN OLD
MEANDER

CAIRO

OLD
MEANDER MARKS

"That's easy!" said Linda. "See, Pat!"

"You look it!" chuckled Bill. "But relax. All hunched up, you'll get stiff. Now you're a turtle, under this boat. Silt is sifting down through the water. That clay on your nose came from Wyoming; sand on your neck, from a Colorado gold mine; your feet stand in Iowa and Illinois cornfields; your shell holds dust from the high Rocky Mountains, and from somebody's level lawn in West Virginia. . . . Now, PRESTO! You're a girl again! . . . You saw a lot of soil going past you, down there. How much do you think the River carries to dump in the Gulf below New Orleans, every year?"

"Must be bushels of it!" said Linda. "I wonder if turtles get stiff necks?"

"Bushels!" cried Patricia. "More like truckloads! Miles of trucks, maybe!"

"Truckloads is right!" said Bill. "It would take six-ton truckloads, lined up bumper to bumper *from here to the moon* — to carry the Mississippi's load, every year! Even now, the low water is muddy. But in floods it's 'too thick to drink, too thin to plow' as the saying goes. And floods not only eat farms, but people and towns!

"Folks started fighting this River over two hundred years back. They built levees around New Orleans to wall off the floods. Next, planters along the River laid out levees to protect their plantations. There were 'levee wars' — gangs from one bank blowing up levees on the other to spill floods away from their own. Now the Government's Army Engineers plan and build and guard all dams and levees. We *hope* the floods will run through cutoffs and spillways without destroying people and land."

"Goodness! And it looks like such a peaceful old river!" said Linda. "I wonder what turtles do in a flood? I'll bet they feel pretty wet all over! I wonder —— "

Minn stirred in the shadows under the boat. Parts of twenty states swirled from her back. She was a bit tired of the River, and its storms of silt. The next week she climbed a levee, and found a pond in an old bend. Long ago the shifty river had deserted its banks and a steamboat, to find a new bend. But many people were glad. They lived on the levees and in the steamboat. Even Minn was happy in her pond.

62

Holling

NEW MADRID
HICKMAN
KY.
TENN.
REELFOOT LAKE
CARUTHERSVILLE
HELOISE
MO
ARK
HALES PT.
OPEN LAKE
LUXORA
ASHPORT
OCEOLA
FULTON
WILSON
RICHARD-SONS
STATE PARK
WOLFE
MEMPHIS
TENN.

SNAGS

"SAWYER"   "DEADHEAD" "PLANTER" "WOODEN ISLAND"

15. BOATS THAT CHANGED THE RIVER

THE next summer, Minn moved from the pond to a sunken steamboat near New Madrid. Time was when this elegant craft toted precious people and freight on the River. By day she was all foamy bustle behind, foam lace at her throat, with two feather boas of smoke tossed over her shoulders. Waving sudden kerchiefs of steam she had called out her coming — till the banks caught the booming billows of sound and bounced them around the bends. By night she turned into a fantastic cake, aglow from within — a platter of white-frosted layers set on black satin. And gaily dressed dancers half hidden inside spun like dolls on a turntable, swirling to chimes and music.

Old Mississippi cared nothing at all whether steamboats floated or sank. Ice on the Upper River crunched a few into splinters, Middle Mississippi sank others with shoals, Lower River and Gulf hurricanes scattered many in swamps. Boilers blew up in tornadoes of steam, draping white wooden lacework across the shuddering trees. Boats burned like volcanoes, erupting in rubies, opals and garnets on gold-plated water. Snags reared from the bottom to rip them open. Snorting breezes snapped them on rocks. Fogs fooled them into colliding. Some duck-paddled through flooded barnyards, seeking the River, squatting like misplaced castles in cornfields when the floods went down. Others met sandbanks where channels had been — slid into deep water, sank — and were forgotten. Minn's sandpile held a few relics. . . .

In different days, Indians rode Missi-Sepe in different kinds of craft. A man could swim it, pushing a log with his moccasins tied in the branches. Roping two logs together gave him a raft, though a tippy one. A hide-covered basket of lashed saplings made a BULLBOAT — a tub for ferrying several men; when empty, a girl could portage it over her head. CANOE frames were sheathed with birchbark in the north, or inner bark of elm where birch did not grow, or with sewn skins. Some tribes made DUGOUTS by burning logs, chipping and digging the charcoal away, smoothing the seasoned, hardened wood with sandstone. A dugout could be heavy, clumsy and slow — or a thin-walled, graceful PIROGUE, "fit to skim the country in a heavy dew!"

TWO-LOG RAFT

BULL-BOAT

64

DUGOUT

PIROGUE (PEER-ŌG')

FLATBOATS WERE "ARKS" OR "BROADHORNS".

FLATBOATS DRIFTED DOWN RIVER, BUT KEELS AND BARGES MOVED UPSTREAM ON MUSCLE!

White men paddled swift Indian craft, but their *freight* moved by FLATBOAT, KEELBOAT and BARGE. The raft-like flatboats floated *down*stream. Round-bottomed "keels" worked slowly *up*stream by poling. Barges were overgrown keels, carrying up to a hundred tons. Though keels and barges had sails, they relied on man-muscle; muscle to row at the bow, tow on the bank, and pole-pole-pole forever!

Most any young men with minds to could drift downriver. On a raft or a flatboat, with a lean-to on it, you sizzled your fish on a sand-box fire as you floated along. Far-off New Orleans was calling; calling for the logs and boards of your craft; for beaver fur, coon pelts and buckskins; for wheat flour, corn meal, hog and bear fat, combs of wild honey and hick'ry nut oil. Aye, you could sell your kit and caboodle, and really *see* New Orleans! Then you could walk home on forest-dark Injun trails, as most fellows did; or by a Cajun pirogue, paddling back north the way you came. But shucks — paddle all that way for nothin'? That there River was all uphill! Why not hire out on a hundred-foot, forty-man barge?

So you *rowed*. Aye, up at the bow, you blistered your ham-sized hands. And you towed. Aye, *how* you *towed!* The thousand-foot tow-cable fast at the mast-top cleared snags and tall brush below — while you barge-men hauled it like mules on a towpath worn deep on the beaches, the banks and the riverside hills. And you *poled*. Aye, up endless muddy reaches. Close-bunched, you all jabbed setting-poles to the bottom; bent over, you nigh pushed your gizzards past eyebrows treading bow-to-stern on the cleated "running boards". You "walked the boat" to the stern, up-hauled poles, ran back and started over. Week on blistered week! *Why* did you *ever* drift *down*stream?

Yet it wasn't enough that you rowed and towed and broke your back at poling. You were young, and the fires danced high on shore, so you dandies danced all night to fiddle-tunes! With the nearest gals forty mile off, what matter? Half the crew wore hats, half were bare-head partners! Tough as stags, graceful as panthers, you pranced and whooped and scared the sleeping crows. Aye — crows *and* people! No wonder timid folk, not liking noise, built their snug homes *back* from the rivers!

THE NIMBLE DUCK

GUNWALE
CLEAT
RUNNING BOARD

THE RIVERMAN WAS "HALF HORSE, HALF ALLIGATOR"

ROWING

TOWING

POLING

BARGE

KEELBOAT

KEEL

HELMSMAN RESTS DURING POLING.

POLING AND RETURNING.

HE CAN STEER ONLY WHILE POLES ARE UP.

65

TOWING OR "CORDELLING" A KEELBOAT

TOWPATH

A HIGH TOWLINE IS ABOVE BRUSH AND SNAGS

KEELBOAT TIPPED TO SHOW BENCHES

③ SIDE-WHEELERS GREW HIGHER, BECAME GLITTERING PALACES BUILT DECK ON DECK LIKE CAKES.

② CAPTAIN HENRY SHREVE BUILT A SHALLOW HULL FOR THE RIVER, SET HIS ENGINES ON DECK, WHICH ALSO HELD CARGO. PASSENGERS SLEPT ON A RAISED DECK, THE "TEXAS".

① EARLIEST STEAMBOATS CARRIED ENGINES LOW, IN SAILING-SHIP HULLS.

SIDE-WHEEL PACKET

SOME BOATS LOOKED LIKE DUCKS.

STERN-WHEEL PACKET

"LANDING STAGES" TO LET DOWN AT THE LANDING

④

PACKETS CARRIED CARGO AND PASSENGERS.

⑤ A COTTON BOAT. ONE BOAT MADE A RECORD CARRYING 9226 BALES.

⑥ STEAMBOATS COULD BE WIDE FOR THE "BIG OLD RIVER".

⑦ STEAMBOATS COULD BE SO SMALL AND NARROW, THEY TRAVELED "ITTY-BITTY BACK BRANCHES. AN' IF THEY STUCK, JES' TIP OVER A RAIN-BAR'L AN FLOAT 'EM OFF TH' MUD."

Yep, 'twas 1811 that changed things. Plenty! Some folks up at Pittsburgh had whanged out an iron kettle, all crawling with pipes; wrestled it into a boat; set a fire under it. A *sane* man would have bet that fool boat would blow to thunder! Yet she could spank herself *up*stream! And she traveled Ohio and Mississippi, out-whooping loudest Injuns and keel-men! Oak-tough pole-men sure hated like poison to admit that horny hands, leather lungs, rawhide sinews were beat by hatfuls of wispy STEAM!

STEAMBOATS changed the rivers — planted new towns, and people. Like keelboats, they had their days of glory. Then came "steam cars." Now other cars, rolling on rubber, coax old steamboat towns to new highways, back from the waterfront; while all-steel TOWBOATS, with "screws" and no paddle-wheels, *push* barges instead of *towing*! Seems like the world's been crazy since 1811, when that first steamboat hit the River!

Yep, Ole Mississip sure went crazy that year! New Madrid Earthquake, worst in U.S. history, rocked the frontier. Lightning flashes, choking sulphur fumes, thundering roars, folks screaming, fowls screeching, cattle bawling — seemed like the end of the world! There were cabins crumbling, folks dying, earth-cracks gaping and swallowing things. Tree-rows leaned back, whipped over, crashed down — and the billows rolled through forests, across solid fields like waves on the liquid sea. . . .

And the River? It sucked itself dry from banks and bed, pulling itself apart. It slammed tons of barges on bare river bed at New Madrid, and the crews ran for shore on sand bottom. Some made it — but the River came back, twelve feet tall, to scoop the wrecks under and race uphill for whole minutes. New Madrid sank some fifteen feet. The earth shuddered, off and on, a couple of years. Even cows got used to staggering. The crazy river had made big Reelfoot Lake, south of Hickman, where no lake was before. That steamboat? Slid down to New Orleans in safety. Old Injuns said its bad magic made the quake! Howsomever, steamboats *did* change the River. . . .

Minn, swimming among her sunken staterooms like a serving platter carried by unseen hands, did not know that the long-ago earthquake had heaped her sandpile.

66

RIVERMAN'S RETREAT

MEMPHIS
TENNESSEE
WEST
MEMPHIS
ARK.

ARK.
TENN.
MISS.

BRUINS

WHITE
HALL

CUTOFF
IN 1874

CUTOFF
IN 1942

ST.
FRANCIS
RIVER

HELENA
ARKANSAS

TENNESSEE

MISSISSIPPI

16. LAND OF COTTON AND TURTLE STEW

AMONG famous old steamboat towns of the Lower River is Memphis, Tennessee. Drawn up from the floods on its bluffs, tall towers of this city loom like shining clouds on the sky. And clouds made Memphis — fluffy clouds of cotton. Cotton-bale-loaded steamboats once crowded Memphis landings. Today's slow freight is trundled by towboats, while cotton chugs by train. But, though busy with many new things besides cotton, Memphis is still called "Cotton-King."

Minn knew cotton. She had seen endless miles of its snowy bushes. At Oceola, Arkansas, waddling into a cotton-gin at night — what a tussle! It clung to claws! It wasn't easy to spit out! But not knowing about Memphis and cotton, Minn lingered awhile. . . .

A white-haired Negro talked with tourists. "Was de South *always* de 'Land of Cotton' — like in de song? No suh! 'Fore a cotton-gin got invent, combin' de li'l seeds away, dey was all picked out by hand — mighty slow work! De South growed jes' 'nuff cotton to dress herself neat. She growed corn, taters, an' such. An' tobaccah, shipped outa New Orleans. When de worl' want blue dye fo' cloth, de South growed indigo plants fo' dye. An' sugah cane! all sugah was brown, till down in New Orleans dey cook up *white* sugah — so everybody plant cane. Den come cotton-gins, an' miles of cotton bales on levees, an' dis was 'Land of Cotton' *sure!* De South sort of clumb a laddah on rungs of tobaccah, indigo, cane an' cotton. An' *now* indus-trees!

"Changes? Yassah! When Ah was young, wild-pigeons flew ovah by de millions! Ah seen flocks of parroty birds, too, like green jewels — 'paroquets.' An' egrets, so many it looked like even swamps growed cotton. In de swamps Ah heard egrets croakin' jes' like frogs; an' frogs bawlin' like bulls; an' bull alligators roarin' like lions. . . .

"Dis rivah, he seen me grow strong. Ah rolled five-hund'ed-pound cotton bales jes' like nothin' — down de levee, 'crost de stage, 'long de steamboat decks — BRUMP-DE-BOMBO, BRUMP-DE-BUMP, like drums. An' we *sung*, dem days. Whut's lef' to sing 'bout now? De pigeons an' paroquets — gone fo'evah. Egrets thinned out. Steamboats almos' gone. . . . But de Rivah, he say 'HOL' TIGHT, BRIGHT DAYS COMIN' BY-'N-BY!'"

COTTON "BALES," ABOUT 500 POUNDS OF COTTON, BURLAP COVERED, PRESSED AND BOUND.

COTTON "BOLLS" (BOWLS), FILLED WITH WHITE FLUFF HOLDING TINY SEEDS. THE "COTTON GIN" COMBS OUT THE SEEDS, USED FOR OIL AND STOCK FEED. THE COTTON MAKES DRESSES, OVERALLS, SHIP SAILS AND QUITE A FEW OTHER THINGS.

"PASSENGER PIGEON" (NOW EXTINCT) LENGTH TO 18 IN.

PRESENT DAY "MOURNING DOVE" LENGTH TO 13 IN.

68

"LOUISIANA PAROQUET" (OR "PARAKEET") 13 INCHES LONG. GREEN WITH YELLOW HEAD. IT ONCE FLEW IN FLOCKS NORTH TO THE SOUTHERN GREAT LAKES. NOW THOUGHT TO BE EXTINCT.

"AMERICAN EGRET" LENGTH UP TO 40 IN.

BUFFALOFISH

"BROWN CATFISH"
"HORNED POUT"
OR "BULLHEAD"

CHANNEL CAT

SHRIMP
OR
"PRAWN"

A FRENCH WORD
FOR A CRAB —
"E'-CRE-VISSE"
(AY-CRAY-VEES),
TWISTED INTO
ENGLISH, IS NOW
"CRAY FISH"
OR
"CRAWFISH".
WE AMERICANS
ADDED
"CRAW DAD".

IN DRY PLACES
CRAWFISH DIG WELLS
DOWN TO WETNESS.
BROILED CRAWFISH IS AN
EXPENSIVE LUXURY IN
THE FINEST RESTAURANTS.

Minn trusted her river, took it for granted — and it was a good provider. She had long known the taste of common bullhead. Down here its cousin, the channel catfish, and another animal-named fish, the buffalo, were delicious. But an old channel cat of two hundred pounds was too big for Minn. She also kept clear of the alligator gar, a five-foot, bony-scaled fish with jaws like an alligator's. Another creature named for the alligator, with gaping mouth but no teeth at all, was Minn's first cousin. Cousin or not, Minn claimed no kin to this alligator snapping turtle. She cruised right on past. She preferred to live with dainty fresh-water shrimp, the always-tasty crawfish, big frogs and fat fishes found in shore pools. After floods drained away they lived between wing-dams, in lagoons or half-moon, horseshoe lakes which had once been bends in the River. . . .

Many miles below Memphis, two Negro boys explored the banks of a lagoon. One grumbled, "All right, Sam! So I'm from the North, and I don't know your South or your old river! But I *do* know your dog has sure been messing with skunks!"

"Cousin Robert," drawled Sam, "does you stay on wif us dis summer, you goin' git close acquainted wif that dawg's smells. That dawg got valuable parts, he has. His full-blood bulldog part never gives up, so he's *always* feudin' wif skunks. Now his full-blood pointer part's showin'. Lookit 'im point!"

The yellow dog balanced on driftwood, staring into the shallows. Sam sauntered over, reached suddenly and scrambled back, dragging a hissing Minn by the tail.

"*What* a *whopper!*" squealed Robert. "What an *ugly, evil*-looking turtle!"

"Evil? She ain't evil — she jes' a snappy tuttle. Your own fault, does you git in her way. A whopper? Ugly? You jes' wait. Now fetch me 'at pole."

In a few excited moments Minn's twenty-five pounds dangled helplessly, her tail tied to a pole carried on the two boy's shoulders. A fearful yelp from the yapping cur, and Minn's head snapped back with a tuft of yellow hair in her jaws.

"Too bad," grunted Sam. "Jes' one more insult he wun't never fergit, besides skunks. Soon he wun't have time fer eatin' — keepin' up with insults an' feuds."

69

THE FEMALE ALLIGATOR, UNLIKE MOST REPTILES, GUARDS HER 3-INCH, OBLONG EGGS BURIED DEEPLY IN A MOUND OF HEAPED-UP RUSHES, LEAVES AND TWIGS.

THE GAR FISH (OR GAR PIKE) IS ONE OF OUR OLDEST FISHES. IT IS A "GAN'-OID" WITH BONY PLATES INSTEAD OF SCALES. IT IS TRULY AN ANCIENT, DESTRUCTIVE AND VICIOUS MONSTER FROM A SAVAGE PAST. ALLIGATOR GARS GROW TO TEN FEET.

Sam and Robert followed the riverbank, Minn swung from the pole like a frying pan and a yellow noise spinning in circles was the dog. When the boys stopped to rest, Minn struck again. This time she seemed to be growing a yellow mustache.

"That dawg goin' be full-blood hairless, mighty soon," Sam sighed. "Now, past them bushes — now over this chicken wire — there you go, Tuttle, to th' puddle."

"But she shies *away* from the puddle!" said Robert. "What's *in* that pond?"

"Look down from here," said Sam, walking around to a plank pushed over the water like a diving board. "That big lump down there is a 'loggerhaid.' Named 'cuz his haid is like th' end of a log, I reckon. But a travelin' man, he say to Pappy, '*Real* loggerhaids is sea-tuttles, like in th' Gulf. This is a *alligator* tuttle.' But Pappy say, 'We got 'gator gar-fish, they kills good fish. We got real 'gators in swamps, they eats hawgs. Ah jes' don' wanna hear no mo' 'bout *'gators!* In this here fambly, this here tuttle is jes' plain *loggerhaid!*'

"Pappy an' Gran'pap, they caught him in th' swamp, fetched him by wagon. He more'n two foot wide, over a hundred pound, too big fer a swill-bar'l — so we made this tuttle-pen. When we turned him loose in it, Pappy stepped on his back, an' he walked off with Pappy to th' puddle, easy! Pappy held a crotch stick to chuck his haid down, did he snap backward. That haid's eight inches wide — could snap Pappy's foot clean off, one bite! He goin' be a big kettle of stew at a County Fair come fall. An' you thought that li'l ole snapper was a *whopper,* huh? Why Robert, 'longside that big ole loggerhaid she's a itty-bitty, gentle kitten!"

That night, painful yelps called the family from the cabin to the turtle pen.

"*That dawg!*" yelled Sam, pointing to a hole under pushed-up wire. "Feudin' agin'! Dug under to git that snapper, but *she* come *out!* Yaller hair all aroun' ——"

"BOTH TUTTLES GOT LOOSE!" bellowed Gran'pap. "CRAWLED UNDER DE FENCE! IF'N DAT WAS *MY* DAWG ——" But that dog was now a full-blooded pointer again. Down at the riverbank, like a statue set on a plank, his nose was pointed at disappearing bubbles.

ANYONE REALLY INTERESTED IN TURTLES SHOULD READ "TURTLES OF THE UNITED STATES AND CANADA" BY CLIFFORD H. POPE.

70

MINN

THE ALLIGATOR SNAPPER, CALLED "LOGGERHEAD"

THE REAL LOGGERHEAD OF THE SEA

ARKANSAS MISS.
WEST HELENA
HELENA
MOON
LAKE
OLD TOWN
DELTA
ELAINE
FRIAR PT.

JACKSON
CUT-OFF 1944
SUNFLOWER
CUT-OFF
1942

LAGRUE
BAYOU
WHITE
RIVER
SNOW
LAKE

ARKANSAS
RIVER
ROSEDALE

FLOWING PAST
PINE BLUFF,
LITTLE ROCK,
FT. SMITH,
IN ARKANSAS;
MUSKOGEE
AND TULSA
IN OKLAHOMA;
ARKANSAS CITY,
WICHITA, HUTCHINSON,
GREAT BEND, DODGE CITY,
GARDEN CITY, SYRACUSE,
IN KANSAS; GRANADA, LAMAR,
LAS ANIMAS, LA JUNTA (HOON-TA),
ROCKY FORD, PUEBLO, CAÑON CITY
AND THE GREAT ROYAL GORGE, SALIDA,
BUENA VISTA, LEADVILLE — (FAMOUS
MINING TOWN SINCE GOLD WAS FOUND
HERE IN 1859) ALL IN COLORADO. AND
NEAR LEADVILLE, TWO MILES HIGH IN
A NEST OF ROCKY MOUNTAIN PEAKS,
THIS GREAT RIVER STARTS ITS 2,000
MILE JOURNEY TO THE MISSISSIPPI
AND THE SALTY SEA.

A "SLOW FLOOD" MAY COME
WHEN THE SWOLLEN RIVER
BACKS UP A SIDE STREAM
FINDS A WEAK LEVEE, AND
OVERFLOWS THE LAND.

17. MINN GOES INLAND

MINN met two kinds of flood on this river — a fast kind, and a slow. A slow flood aroused her from winter sleep a mile up a side stream. Swollen Mississippi waters backed up this stream from its mouth, crept across fields, reached the levee again on its landward side. Thus a slow, silent flood lay alongside a raging river, dry levee-top between — a pitiful ribbon of land threading a desert of waters.

At first, sleepy Minn was pushed by the slow flood. She bumped through woods where raccoons, opossums, terrified bobcats clutched at trees. Cows, knee-deep in water, could find no dry standing place. Minn rolled down a road where cars sputtered and died, their drivers wading away. At a two-floor-and-attic house, far back from the crowded levee, she hid behind iron kettles on a flooded porch. Rowboats came bringing dogs, old folks, children, women, men. These "johnboats" also brought bedding, boxes, pots, pans, banjos, guitars. That night the candlelit house was gay with plunked-up courage.

Next day, scows brought chickens, pigs, calves, a baby mule. Minn and the flood had now moved well inside. Surfacing near a row of monstrous white teeth, Minn left that piano to dive under a stove. Boys swam gleefully toward stairs. Little girls stared from johnboats coming through windows. A baby splashed under in streams of bubbles, but scrawny arms snatched him up before he sank to the floor.

Next day Minn bumped the ceiling. She fought through festoons of sagging wallpaper and paddled out to the porch roof. The house was noisy, but not with music. From an upper window floated an un-glued guitar. Minn followed lazily. . . .

She returned to find only a tent-shaped roof above water. A man at the attic window shot swimming snakes — but other snakes crawled un-seen upon the roof. An oar burst upward through shingles, waving a diaper. A big boat turned among tree tops toward it, joining itself to the attic window with planks. Minn left the glad noises to go below, where even the snarling piano now sat smothered in silt. When she surfaced again, the rescued people were gone. Two sopping, exhausted panthers slept on a bed by the attic window. Beside them, contentedly rat-filled, four cotton-mouth snakes lay coiled. . . .

72

That was a slow flood. People had whole hours to prepare for it. But two years after, while wintering in an old muskrat tunnel bored into the levee, Minn was caught up in a fast flood. Though the tunnel was hidden from men by weeds, the spring rise found and started carving it into a cave. Swirling currents sloshed around in it. The growling river rose higher, attacking a whole mile of levee, gouging Minn's burrow wider and deeper; but Minn still clung to it.

Sleepy Minn grew slowly aware of thuds and vibrations. She could not guess that hundreds of tired men toiled above her. They staggered along with loaded wheelbarrows, and piled sandbags like heavy building blocks to hold the levee. Bags thudded by dozens. Some spilled into the River, slid to Minn's cave and pinned her there. She did not feel buried, but safe. She settled back to her snooze. . . .

Though men heaped bags by thousands, by tons, none knew what went on below. By dismal day and lantern-lit night men moved like mechanical toys, wound up to pat back the River. But the small, slow toys were not enough. They were running down, while the River was rising — rising — a Dragon lashing its tail, heaving its body higher, licking at the levee-top. "GET OUT! FOR YOUR LIVES!" . . . Slime-covered humans slid and scrambled away. . . .

Now the Dragon really writhed in its cave. Walls came away like wet sugar at each mad whirl. A mass of sandbags dropped through the cave roof in seething foam. Narrow torrents gushed through the dike. All its earth shuddered. Then a mile-long, dirty-white wall rolled over the levee, scraped it away in thundering sweeps and billowed down toward the low, flat land.

Sandbags were no longer heavy blocks. Those holding Minn flew up and outward like wind-tossed leaves, taking Minn with them. In this bellowing liquid she struck a post, a telephone pole, a shed wall. But even as she struck, these solid things sagged like pillows and disappeared. Because she bumped too many things along the bottom, Minn fought to the surface. Across open country she sped like a surfboard, ten feet above fields. She struck a train but the boxcars fell over, tossing and wallowing after her, like playful whales. Trees went down, leaped up and rushed forward like shaggy beasts crazed by fear. . . .

73

THE "FAST FLOOD" CAME WHEN THE LEVEE BROKE AND A WALL OF WATER RUSHED MINN WITH IT ACROSS THE LOW FLAT LAND.

When the shuddering wall of water first tumbled upon them, land creatures were stunned. They had no time even to feel afraid. Fear would come to them in the faraway future — one second — two seconds — three long seconds from now. Fear and death would come later — and would linger — and would last. But right now everything joined this parade of mad liquid motion dancing and prancing away. . . .

There was something quite gay in the way barns and houses sprang up and waltzed off on the water. In one rush, settled things of a township swirled toward other counties. Towns tottered off under see-sawing, teetering roofs. Wooden house-walls wobbled apart, slapping down rafts neatly painted, papered and strewn with framed pictures. Some rafts broke up into timbers and boards — and the boards into splinters. People owned these possessions no more. The River had swiftly snatched and robbed. The robbing River held everything. . . .

At last the prancing push went out of the water. It stopped going somewhere. It flattened out. It was still. It was still, and its thick wash of mud clung to all it touched. Then the mud-water sea began sinking and shrinking. It grew stagnant. It smelled of dead things strewn on the brush and the clay-washed fences. The smell was a silent call to vultures and crows. They shook themselves out of lead-pudding clouds and plopped into ghost-gray trees. They ate where they sat and slept where they ate, too lazy to trust their new weight to winter-worn wings. . . .

Minn was tired. No turtle can roll across country like a three-spoked wheel without feeling weary. She had come to the edge of a tipped-over barn, and clung to it in a dazed way. There were ducks on the barn's sloping side, two pigs and a very sad mule. The mule munched soaked hay pulled through a hole in the siding. The ducks were not swimming. Of late, even ducks had seen too much water. . . .

The still, dead water sank down. That summer, it all dribbled away. Minn followed its dribblings, from puddle to drying puddle, with crows for company. When she met the River again, it had gouged a new course for itself in its ancient mud.

74

ARK./MISS.

ARK.
RIVER
ROSE
DALE
CHALK
CUT-OFF
1937
ARKAN-
SAS
CITY
SCOTT
TARPLEY
CUT-OFF
1935
LELAND
CUT-OFF
1933
GREEN-
VILLE
LAKE
VILLAGE
WAYSIDE
AMERICAN
CUT-OFF
1938
EUDORA
CHATHAM
ARK.
LA.
GRAND LAKE
CUT-OFF
1796-1817
SARAH CUT-OFF
1936
POSSUM
CHUTE
ROLLING
FORK
MAYERS
VILLE
LAKE
PROVIDENCE
TALLULA
FITLER
INDIAN
MOUNDS
WILLOW
CUT-OFF
1934
YAZOO
BLUFFS
YAZOO
CUT-OFF
1799
CENTENNIAL
CUT-OFF 1876
VICKS-
BURG
(HEADQUARTERS
OF MISS. R. COMMISSION
CORPS OF ARMY ENGIN-
EERS - GUARDIAN OF
ALL RIVER WORK ON
THE LOWER MISS. R.)
DIAMOND CUTOFF 1933
BIG BLACK R.
HARD
TIMES
BEND
HARD
SCRABBLE
BEND
GRAND GULF
BAYOU PIERRE
LAKE
BRUIN
ST.
JOSEPH
PORT GIBSON
WATER
PROOF
RODNEY
RODNEY CUTOFF
1936
COLES CREEK
FIELDS
LAKE
FAYETTE
BLUFFS
GILES CUT-OFF 1933
NATCHEZ

18. RIVER OF DREAMS

On this river, man-made things were small. Minn drifted in such wide, gold-brown space, that a smoking chip of steamboat scarcely seemed to move. Its far music spread out softly, unraveling one melody into many — akin to all tunes, over all waters everywhere. . . . But the boat grew into two, one pushing the other; and its music, boomed from a steam calliope, shrieked one tune for miles.

Most tow-boats Minn had met pushed such things as coal and steel. This one pushed a white barge loaded with dreams — a "showboat." At a river town, cars clattered toward it, mules dragged buggies, boys galloped horses, big crowds came. Tickets let humans walk a plank bridge to a dazzling, make-believe world. Here long-dead kings lived again, on a stage. Here ladies were ladies, villains were punished, old jokes came in new clothes. Under this showboat, Minn settled down.

During some plays the boat was hushed and still. Some plays brought laughter. Laughter rippled like breezes over the water, it came in squalls, and sometimes Minn was fairly roofed with thunder. She was vaguely puzzled — but she still knew *hooks*. Between shows, when armored knights fished from the rail, and costumed ladies dangled catfish bait, Minn gave such acts a cold, reptilian stare. . . . She was mildly sorry when the showboat vanished, taking along its tickling vibrations. But humans who had watched its plays carried bright dreams to lonely cabins. Memories of laughter added flavor to grits, hominy, salt pork and hot corn pone. . . .

Mile on mile, year after year, Minn ate and drifted down a wider River, across flatter land. Bluffs — worn old shores of the ancient Gulf, now lost to the eastward, would not return till Vicksburg. But here and there, beyond the levee walls — higher than swamps, or fields, or cabins, or big houses with columns, or even forest trees — Minn sometimes saw strange hills. Here also the Mound Builders had left monuments to forgotten dreams, heaping them up on the flatness of the land. They were promises that, when waters raged again, these lonely humps of earth would remain standing; islands of refuge against a river forever changing its mind.

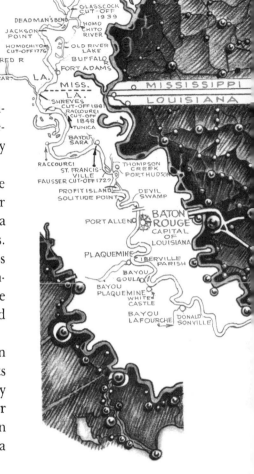

Golden sunlight played on the River, and ghosts of gold wandered this flat land. Minn found a rusted Spanish sword above Rosedale and the Arkansas River. From what young hand in De Soto's army had this sword dropped, ending a dream? . . .

In 1539, De Soto's army hoped to find gold in Florida. But the dream turned into a nightmare. North — south — north and west — for three years it haunted them. On this wild stage, Indians provided drama — but no gold. Fighting Indians was like fighting fog with swords. True, Spaniards had crossbows and cannon — but in tangled swamps their aim was poor. Natives scuttled like quail in the weeds, and vanished. But their stone points pierced steel armor! Spaniards were wounded in empty forests while laughter cackled, roared and echoed among the moss-hung trees. . . .

Yet De Soto *did* find something golden — a Great River, golden with mud in the sun. And he crossed the River, and he died of its fevers; and they slid his body beneath its golden coils. . . . But why should the River remember? How can a river remember a dream — or buzzards and crows hovering over an army — or a bearded man in an oak log coffin, weighted and sinking down? . . . And what could a rusted sword lost from this dream ever mean to Minn? . . .

Bluffs found the River again at Vicksburg. And Minn found other weapons and tools which had helped in the fight to develop a great South. There were also mud-silenced cannon which had once argued. But what could Minn know of struggles of dreams on a giant stage — or a heroic act entitled "Siege of Vicksburg?" . . .

And the bluffs were at Natchez. . . . Natchez bluffs, too, remembered. They held memory of graceful columns, gleaming mansions, stately trees and stately people beneath them. Natchez held gentleness and grace from another time. But the grace had the strength of steel behind it. Natchez, too, had left swords in the River. . . .

And Baton Rouge. . . . Even its name held a memory — of a "Red Stick" set as an Indian boundary. Now Minn had passed through two state capitals — a northern St. Paul, a Baton Rouge of the South — linked by the same river. . . . Minn saw many ships at Baton Rouge. They screeched and moaned their coming in strange tongues. Their steel bottoms were bumpy with barnacles gathered in far-off seas. . . .

77

NATCHEZ HOLDS THE SPELL
OF "THE OLD SOUTH."
MANY OF HER MANSIONS
NOT ONLY DATE BACK, BUT
KEEP THE SPIRIT OF "DAYS
BEFORE THE WAR."
WHAT WAR? A NORTHERNER WOULD SAY
"THE CIVIL WAR", A SOUTHERNER "THE WAR BETWEEN THE STATES."

The River brought Minn to Nine Mile Point in the dusk. Across, on the left, lay New Orleans. Here, for two centuries and a half, pirogues, rafts, flatboats, keel boats — shantyboats, barges, steamboats, towboats — had slowed down to seek the banks. They had reached home. . . . But Minn steered away from the sides of this trough, and held to mid-channel. Behind those levees sprawled New Orleans, a walled city, a panful of city below the River's rim. And somehow Minn sensed that New Orleans knew all about pots and pans; that here, more than most places in the world, humans seemed to have an instinct for seasoning fat turtles. Minn kept going. . . .

New Orleans is a cooking pan — and a laughing face above it. It is the face of numberless ancestors who came from afar to reach this River. They came from lands across the sea — from Europe, from Africa, from Asia. Yet some ancestors were already here when those others came. Indians have looked longest at this river. . . . Like its mingled waters, the laughing face of New Orleans is the face of America. . . .

New Orleans is a cooking pan, a laughing face — and a rhythm. A soft humming runs down its levees like rain-trickles of sound. It comes from houses, mansions, shops and skyscrapers; from dark alleys and day-bright boulevards; from people working and people at play; from feet hissing on dance floors, from hands beating, from singing mouths; and the rhythm is cradled in crooning strings, a moaning of trumpets, drums sobbing. . . . And some of the rhythm has jungle in it; it tells of other rivers, crocodiles, long cats and shadows of elephants. . . . And as Minn went by, drums talked this New Orleans rhythm into the river-night. . . .

And so Minn left this first — or last — big city on the River. She left the cooking pan, the laughing face, the haunting rhythm. . . . And the rhythm became the beat of steamboats — then two oars rowing — then a whispering wavelet at the bow of a pirogue. Behind Minn New Orleans, ablaze like a continuous carnival, became a thin line of lights, a twinkling memory — and then the stars took over. As in some dream, it seemed that stars fell down — to glow in dim, green fires deep in the River. . . .

78

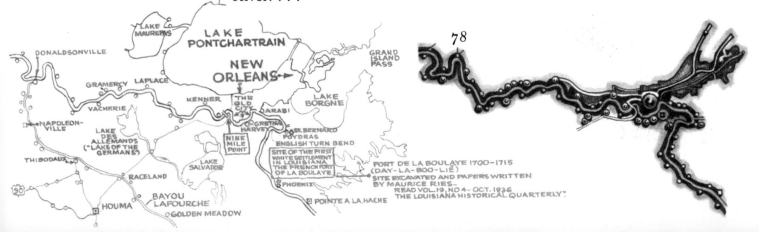

19. MINN COMES TO THE END OF THE LINE

After twenty-five well-fed summers, Minn was fat and content with life. Year by year she had given in more to the River. Surely it ran on forever. It would always provide. Yet something was wrong in this coffee-colored paradise. It was *too salty!* She was now used to a strange tide flowing upriver for hours at a time, making the water brackish as far upstream as Baton Rouge. But this stuff was just too salty for a fresh-water turtle! She would leave it till that briny taste and smell had washed away!

Once more Minn climbed a levee. Flabby, fat muscles heaved her bulk from a backwash, up and up. She scraped over concrete, and slid down to what she hoped was a fresh-water lagoon. *FRESH* WATER? That liquid was positively *bitter* with salt! . . . What did she know of Southwest Pass — one of the fingers of sand and running water the River pokes into the sea? She had crawled from it only to waddle down to a bay of the briny Gulf itself! Slowly she clambered back the way she had come. . . .

With out-flowing ebb tide and swift current chasing it, Minn picked up speed. She held to center channel, not to be scraped on the jetties at either side. Her flabby muscles could not turn her back. Drifting Minn had come to the end of the line whose Hook of Lakes had hatched her. . . . SLAP — SLAP — SLAP — she was walloped by salty, stinging waves! Minn and her Mississippi had reached the sea. . . .

Others had followed this river to find this sea. First there were Spaniards — wound-weary soldiers. Having buried De Soto and built themselves boats, they followed the River to its end. Perhaps — hugging shore — if luck held with them — they might reach Mexico. . . . Then came Frenchmen. Staunch La Salle had stood on the surf-sand, calling aloud that he claimed this wild land for Louis, his king; the River, its rivers, all the land they drained — "Louisiana". . . . How much land did this mean? La Salle did not know. It did not matter. He had called out words, the seabirds had heard him, the wind in the grass, and the sand. What birds? Long dead. . . . What sand? Long lost to the Gulf. . . . But no matter. Though the words died on the wind, "Louisiana" clung to men's minds and changed the world. . . .

80

BROWN
PELICAN

WHITE
PELICANS

MAN-O'-WAR BIRD

GULLS

BLACK
SKIMMER

PORTUGUESE
MAN-OF-WAR

Sands and grasses melted away behind Minn. The whole North American continent melted away. Minn felt alone in this vast sea of restless, salty waves. Yet she was not alone. Lumbering pelicans, some brown, some black and white; a swallow-tailed cruiser of ocean skies, the man-o'-war-bird; black skimmers, with lower beaks plowing the surface, all flapped at and past her. She saw a cousin of jellyfish, a Portuguese man-of war, like a purple balloon with a fin of sail, trailing long hair-tentacles. A kite-shaped sting-ray slid beneath her, a nightmare in flowing cape. A lazy shark and three slender rem'-o-ra fish turned to look at her. Like scouting pilots, each remora stared and pointed, while the shark smelled Minn with his scow-ended nose. Though he was hungry, as always, he decided against a very doubtful meal. Besides, this horny thing might chip his teeth, or get stuck in his gullet. So he flipped his tail, the remora scouts glued their heads to him, and all glided away. A loggerhead sea-turtle, many times Minn's size, paused to look her over. He hovered, waved aimless flippers, blinked solemn eyes and seemed to be thinking "no close kin of mine." He left Minn to herself again in the Gulf of Mexico.

Minn seldom worried about anything. Yet in all this glaring, salty openness she felt uneasy. The bottom was sand, but much too bright with sunlight — or the bottom was dark silt, sunlight still hammering down. This sand and soil, dumped by the River, would someday fill this entire part of the sea. Minn could not wait that long for a rest, what with waves lifting and slamming her down. Bottom-walking here got her nowhere at all. There was nowhere to hide. So, when uprooted palm trees from Central America hove in view, Minn paddled toward them eagerly. Here was shade! And this tangle of old fronds broke the waves. She scrambled through a network of roots and found a snug resting place. Best of all, bright little crabs and darting fishes lived among the roots. And that meant EATING again!

Next morning the whole sea seemed to know that trouble was brewing. Small fish were worried and swam past in glittering schools. Big fishes were worried and restless. Shapes that Minn had never seen came from nothing and vanished in nothing, nervously. Even Minn wondered what was coming, in her vague snapper way. But the gale struck so swiftly she lost her palm trees, and never saw them again.

81

LOGGERHEAD

STING RAY

THE
STINGER

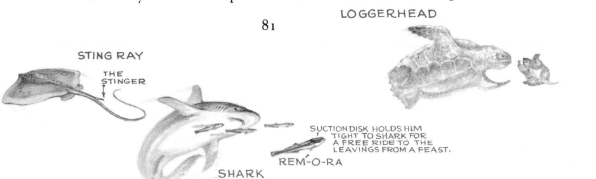

SUCTION DISK HOLDS HIM
TIGHT TO SHARK FOR
A FREE RIDE TO THE
LEAVINGS FROM A FEAST.

REM-O-RA

SHARK

The gale was not a hurricane, but it blew enough for Minn. Warrior waves charged shoreward, rank on rank, tripping and falling while headgear rolled in a froth of plumes. Minn was hurled to the hard sandy bottom, hauled back up, heaved forward like a heavy weight in a shot-put. Not even old Lake Pepin had made her feel so dizzy. She was as nearly seasick as a snapping turtle can be. . . .

After the storm, two Cajun fishermen found her, tossed up on a sand island in Barataria Bay. One cried, "A tired-tired snapper! Beat up by the wind! Help me, Pierre, we lift her in the boat! By the saints! Forty pound, I bet me!"

For hours on end the boat chugged north through grassy marshes. It kicked up birds like insect clouds in a hayfield. Leaving clear, salt water, it came to dark-stained fresh water, winding among trees. From bay to lake, to bayou, to canal, it sputtered and slid to a stop near the gates of a lock. Here was a high levee. Over it, unseen steamers talked in grunts. Minn had completed a grand detour — back to New Orleans!

"Forty-six pounds!" cried a man on the bank as they weighed the snapping Minn.

"Mighty big weight, fer that breed of turtle," drawled an angular woman walking into the crowd. "Hm. Three legs. . . . LUKE, COME HERE! . . . Listen, you with th' turtle! Fer that there fat turtle meat, restaurants crost th' River *might* pay you ten dollars. But *I'll* pay you *twenty!* Yep, twenty. I got that much fer one like that 'un, years back, so I break even. But you wouldn't understand. . . ."

Hours later, the two Cajuns chugged back along the bayous. One stared at blue rafts of water hyacinths beneath the bearded trees, muttering, "In all the newspapers! Now all the country will know we sell a three-leg snapper to a crazy woman! TWENTY DOLLAR she pay — an' only for to *turn it loose!* But we can catch it again, an' sell it to —— "

"No, Pierre. Did you hear folks talkin' 'bout that woman? She shoots a rifle. She shoots a duck dead. Flyin'! One bullet. This boat don't need any *new* holes! That woman, that man, come every few year on a new boat, a new EVANGELINE. She reads 'bout our people. She likes us. I think, maybe, she is not so crazy. . . ."

82

20. TREASURE IS WHERE YOU FIND IT

PIRATES had come to this bayou, long ago, frightening the birds. Snowy egrets swarmed up from the swamp as six pirogues, almost awash with the weight in them, slid to a small island. Bearded men carried chest after heavy chest into bushes, where spades flicked sand from a pit. When the chests were buried, each man backed toward shore, brushing all tracks away with palmetto fans. The boats retreated, and birds returned to their tangles. Hours later, from the Gulf came cannon thunders and rattles of musket fire. Then the swamp sank back to its quiet of dark-stained water, half hidden by hanging curtains of Spanish moss. Nothing remained to show that humans had come here. And those men never returned. . . .

One wild hurricane evening, waves changed the island. They swirled its sand into new spits and patterns, uncovered the nest of many chests, undermined and sank them. New mud slid over them, winged seeds spun down, and one cypress tree grew there. Its big roots pierced rotting, leather-sheathed wood, pried apart iron bands binding the chests. Small rootlets fingered gold pieces-of-eight and polished jewels. . . .

The cypress tree grew old, straddling treasure beneath four feet of water. Its flared-out roots made a barred vault. Currents had many times washed the hoard clean, only to silt it over again. Now Minn made her home here. From a domed palace with buttressed-root columns she sallied forth to hunt — crossing a threshold of rubies, emeralds, diamonds and enough gold coins to ransom princes and kings. . . .

Thus Minn lived on a glittering heap — of what? Rich jewels, once more, were merely stones; and one of earth's heaviest elements — melted neatly into golden wafers of equal weight — was returned again to the care of earth and water. For Minn, her doorstep of so-called treasure was only a hardness, like water-worn pebbles. . . .

Frogs drummed in the bayous. Mosquitoes whined. Alligators roared. A few egrets stood on dark cypress knees, wading herons poked under trailing moss. Swimming mink, otter and muskrats traced thin lines on the surface with vanishing tails. Dark paths of water suddenly rippled, were swiftly still. Air moved with wings. . . .

84

Minn had not noticed the patched old scow. It drifted, slowly turning on the dark bayou. A breeze swung tatters of moss, prodded the waterlogged craft — and died with the effort. When the boat touched the roots of her cave, Minn walked over her silt-covered pavement and drifted slowly upward. Above her, a push-pole leaned from the end of the scow. A white face, topped by carrot-red hair, looked over the side.

"Ah hate tuttles —" muttered the boy, softly. Then he shrieked "TUTTLES! . . . AH HATE *TUTTLES!* AH HATE! AH *HATE! AH HATE! . . .*"

Minn sank quickly, but now came a torrent of blows. The push-pole beat at the twisted roots. It stabbed between them — down, and down again. It jabbed gold coins into the mud. It toppled gold candlesticks, scattered a stack of jeweled swords and sabers, punched through the rim of a golden chalice and burst a small casket of diamonds. Whatever it struck was jarred free of silt, to shimmer and glitter and gleam. While Minn, safe in her root stockade, watched the jerky paths of the pole take fire in the water. . . .

Then it was over. The pole jerked upward, the bayou settled to shadowy calm, but the voice snarled on — "Ah hate ever'thing! . . . Call me pore white trash. Call *me* white trash! Whut if Pappy hain't got no money? He got cricks in th' back. Cain't do nothin' but sleep — an' whup me. . . . But *they* ain't got no right. *They* ain't got th' say of *me!* Jes' wait. Jes' wait till Ah git a MILLION DOLLARS! . . .

"Hey you, ole crow up thar — think you is safe, huh? Jes' wait. With a million dollahs — know whut Ah'd do? Buy me 'at shiny gun Ah seen — an' blow you, Crow, to feathahs so fine they'd sift down like soot! Buy a cannon an' blow up th' bayous, an' all th' folks! . . . But no — that ain't so smart. . . . Buy me a yacht. An' all th' things Ah seen, up to New Orleans. Then they'd butter up! They'd say 'please' to me! . . . An' ah'd go political. They'd vote fer me, if'n Ah was growed. Ah'd be boss an' *they'd* work — AH'D MAKE 'EM WORK *PLENTY!* Ah'd run th' State — maybe git to be *Prezzy-dunt!*" With sudden energy he pushed the johnboat from the tree. "WHY, *AH COULD BOSS TH' WORLD! . . .* If'n Ah had me a measly li'l ole million dollahs! . . ."

85

A graceful pirogue slipped like a shadow beside Minn's cypress. A slender Acadian boy peered past soft curtains of moss.

"I pity him, that one," he said, watching the scow poled jerkily away. "Always he bites — like a scared, sick dog. An' so he wants the million dollars? Millions are here, yes — here in these bayous. Old pirate stories are true. Pirates killed, robbed ships in th' Gulf, buried big treasure in these bayous. Then they died an' couldn't use it. Now it's God's. Grand-Père, he say too many folks go crazy an' die, jus' wishin' an' diggin' and worryin' an' wishin' for treasure. Grand-Père, he is a wise man. He say you find riches only as a gift from God. . . .

"That one in th' scow — will he find a million? Only God knows. An' me — why should *I* find a million? *I* do not need th' treasure buried in God's banks of sand an' mud. That is maybe the great satisfaction. With gold in town banks — does one handle the gold? No. One has the paper money instead. So, Grand-Père he say we Cajuns have the same as buried treasure; stars for diamonds, an' nobody gets killed for them; gold of the shrimp an' the crab from rich waters, the silver of shining fish. Isn't that enough treasure — for us to dig it, any time? For us, that is enough. . . .

"Us Cajuns — we had it tough as any, two hundred years back, to hear Grand-Père tell. When we came down from Canada, did we make the big plantations? No, we took the swamps nobody wanted. Did we sit an' wish for a million dollars? No. We worked. We are still ver' proud of how *hard* we worked! . . . So now, we got ever'thing we need. An' nobody is happy like us! . . .

"Maybe, even, we are happy like this ole turtle. . . . Hey, you down there! You happy? Come up, frien', an' have the talk! Maybe I give you music, with my guitar. You an' me — we got plenty food, good place for livin' — we got th' waters an' th' bright blue sky. An' we just as free as that old crow, flappin' away out there. Grand-Père — he say there is nothin' better than jus' bein' free. . . . Free like that Mississippi beyond those far trees — runnin' forever to the sea. . . ."

THE END